Margaret Oliphant

Memoir of the Life of Laurence Oliphant and of Alice Oliphant, his Wife

Vol. 1

Margaret Oliphant

Memoir of the Life of Laurence Oliphant and of Alice Oliphant, his Wife
Vol. 1

ISBN/EAN: 9783337416171

Printed in Europe, USA, Canada, Australia, Japan

Cover: Foto ©Raphael Reischuk / pixelio.de

More available books at **www.hansebooks.com**

MEMOIR

OF THE

LIFE OF LAURENCE OLIPHANT

AND OF

ALICE OLIPHANT, HIS WIFE

BY

MARGARET OLIPHANT W. OLIPHANT

IN TWO VOLUMES

VOL. I.

NEW YORK

HARPER & BROTHERS, FRANKLIN SQUARE

1891

PREFACE.

I HAVE, in concluding this book, to thank almost
all the persons most closely connected with Laurence Oliphant for their kind confidence in in-
trusting me with the numerous letters which
reveal his character so much more clearly than
anything else can,—especially those which show
the formation of that character, addressed to his
mother in the early part of his life, which I owe
to the courtesy of Mrs Rosamond Oliphant, now
Mrs James Murray Templeton : a courtesy all the
more marked that I believe she herself intended,
or still intends, to make some record, though probably from a different point of view, of her late
husband's life. I have also to render my best
thanks to Mrs Wynne Finch, the mother of the
late Mrs Laurence Oliphant ; to Mrs Waller, her
sister, and to Hamon le Strange, Esq., her brother,
for much most interesting information and a num-

ber of important letters. Other letters have come
to me through Mrs Wynne Finch and other channels—from Lady Guendolen Ramsden, the Hon.
F. Leveson Gower, Major Goldsmid, and others,
to whom my best thanks are also due. I have
also most grateful thanks to give to Mr and
Mrs J. D. Walker, formerly of San Rafael, Cali-
fornia, for an account of many incidents of great
value in the record of the two lives; to Mrs
Hankin, of Malvern, for the use of her notes of
intercourse, both by letter and personally; to
Arthur Oliphant, Esq.; and to Lady Grant Duff,
in whose house Mr Oliphant died.

I have one other acknowledgment to make,
which in happier circumstances would have been
said only to the private ear of him to whom it is
due. A great part of the letters quoted here
were selected, arranged, and connected for me by
my dear son, Cyril Francis Oliphant, whom it
pleased God to take to Himself just as the book
was ended, the last work he did on earth being
included in these pages. It can never bear to
me any other memorial and inscription than his
beloved name. .

December 8, 1890.

CONTENTS OF THE FIRST VOLUME.

CHAPTER I.

HIS PARENTAGE AND CHILDHOOD.

CHAPTER II.

BEGINNING LIFE.

CHAPTER III.

THE BAR—THE EXPEDITION TO RUSSIA.

CHAPTER IV.

AMERICA AND CANADA.

CHAPTER V.

THE CRIMEA.

CHAPTER VI.

THE MISSION TO CHINA.

CHAPTER VII.

POLITICAL ADVENTURE—SOCIAL LIFE.

MEMOIR

LIFE OF LAURENCE OLIPHANT.

———•———

CHAPTER I.

HIS PARENTAGE AND CHILDHOOD.

THE subject of this memoir, Laurence Oliphant, was a man so unique in himself, so entirely individual and distinct in his generation, that it is more than ordinarily unnecessary to distinguish him by the mild and modest honours of the family of Scotch country gentlemen from which he sprang. I may be permitted, however, the natural weakness of some brief notice of the race of which he has proved one of the most distinguished members, and to which I also belong, both by birth on the mother's side and by marriage. The fond superstition of ancient race, to which the Scot in all his developments is prone, may be accepted as an excuse for this unfortunately somewhat vague and not very brilliant passage of history. We have not, I fear, been very remarkable as a race. After the first somewhat misty heroes of the past, the house appears only in the occasional mention of a name here and there,—when a Lord Oliphant witnessed a royal charter, or lent his silent support to a protest or revolt of the Scots nobility of his time. There is a page in a manuscript of the seventeenth century, preserved in the Heralds' College, which sums up their dispositions in words very quaint and graphic, and very satisfactory in the point of view of the domestic virtues, but not, perhaps, indicative of much greatness. "The Lord Oliphant.—This baron," says that anonymous authority, "is not of great renown, but yet he hath good landes and profitable; a house very loyal to the Kings of Scotland; accounted no orators in theyr wordes nor yet foolish in theyr deedes. They do not surmount in theyr alliances, but are content with theyr worshipful neighbours." "As for the antiquity of the family and sirname," says Nisbet in his 'System of Heraldry,' in the chapter which treats of "Celestial Figures; the Sun, Moon, and Stars," to which the bearings of the family belong,

" there was an eminent baron of that name who accompanied King David I. to the siege of Winchester in England in the year 1142, named David de Oliphard; and the same man or another of that name is to be found frequently a witness to that king's charters; and particularly (says Mr Crawfurd, in his 'Peerage') in that to the Priory of Coldingham, whereto his seal is appended, which has thereupon three crescents, which clearly prove him to be the ancestor of the noble family of Oliphant, who still bear the same figures in their ensign armorial."

In the Scottish War of Independence, Sir William Oliphant of Aberdalgy, in Forfarshire, the acknowledged head of the house, held Stirling Castle against the English; but was not, I fear, quite free of the intrigues of the time, and those occasional changes of side which even the great Bruce himself, before he settled into his noble career, was sometimes betrayed into. His son was, however, rewarded for their exertions in the cause of their country by the hand of Elizabeth Bruce, the king's daughter, who was not indeed a legitimate princess—but the distinction counted for little in those days. A generation or two later, the heir of the house acquired some portion of the estate of Kellie in Fifeshire, upon which he settled his second son, Walter Oliphant, my own ancestor, and the founder, it is believed, of the picturesque old house called Kellie Castle, in the rural parish of Carnbee, still standing in perfect repair, and most admirably restored by its late inmate, Professor Lorimer of Edinburgh. The barony was conferred afterwards upon the head of the house in 1467. It was renewed on failure of the direct male line by Charles I. in 1657, and became extinct in 1751. In the meantime the family threw off many branches, one of the latest of which was that of Condie, which bears the three crescents, " within a bordure counter compony gules and argent," and changed the original crest of a Unicorn's head to that of " a Falcon volant," and the old thrifty motto *A Tout pourvoir*, which, I am proud to say, was retained by the Kellie branch, into the newer fashion of a Latin proverb, *Altiora Peto,* of which, the reader will remember, the most brilliant descendant of the house of Condie made in after days a whimsical use.

I am grieved to say that none of the many branches of the house have done anything very remarkable in life. The Jacobite Lairds of Gask have supplied an interesting volume to Scots family history by means of their present representative, Mr Kington Oliphant, whose own achievements in philology and cognate subjects

are not small; and Caroline Oliphant, afterwards Lady Nairne, of the same family, was one
of the band of women-poets, full of the native
music and delightful natural sentiment of their
country, who have left so pleasant and so bright
a tradition behind them. Perhaps no work of
genius ever gained a more universal or delightful
fame for its author than the song, " The Land o'
the Leal," written by this accomplished woman,
has done. Otherwise the record of the name is
like the shield of Sir Torr—void of achievement.
The house of Condie was no exception to this
law: country gentlemen, Scots lawyers, a soldier brother now and then, have maintained the
worthy tradition of one of those plain Scotch
families, in whose absence of distinction so much
modest service to their country is implied. Anthony Oliphant, a second son of the house, went
farther afield than to the Parliament House of
Edinburgh, and found his fortune in the colonies,
where he held various dignified posts. Sixty
years ago he was Attorney-General at the Cape,
where he married Miss Maria Campbell, the
daughter of Colonel Campbell of the 72d High-
landers, and his wife, a member of the large
and important family of Cloete; and there, at
Cape Town, in the year 1829, Laurence was
born. He was the only child of a pair both of

whom were notable in their way : she, full of
the vivacity and character which descended to
her son ; he also a man of much individual power
and originality, an excellent lawyer and trusted
official. Both were deeply stamped with the form
of religious feeling which was most general among
pious minds at the time. There is no scorn of
religion implied in the fact that it too has its
fashions, which shape in successive waves the gene-
rations as they go. This couple were evangelical
in their sentiments, after the strictest fashion of
that devout and much-abused form of faith. The
constant self-examination, the minute and scrupu-
lous record of every little backsliding, the horror
of those gaieties and seductions of the world (much
modified, in fact, by that considerable share in
them which their position made necessary), which
were but too agreeable to the social instincts of
both, is characteristically evident in a letter which
Sir Anthony, then Chief-Justice of Ceylon, addressed to his little son Laurence, ten years old,
at that time in England with his mother, and
whose tender mind the parents were so anxious
to train into the ways of godliness. The glimpse
this letter gives of the natural man, a little warm
of temper, a little rash in ejaculation, underneath
the cloak of the conscientious Christian, who felt
that for every idle word he would be called to

judgment, is, if I may dare to say it, amusing as well as attractive, though the intention of the writer is far removed from any such thought. It is addressed to his dear little boy, who had been very ill, and had just recovered and written his first letter, " very well written and spelt," to his papa. This loving and tender papa had been transferred from the Cape to Ceylon in the absence of his wife and child in England, and describes to his little son his extreme loneliness in arriving at his new post.

"COLOMBO, *May* 31, 1839.

" After mamma and you went away from the Cape to England for mamma's health, mamma asked the great people in England to remove me from being Attorney-General at the Cape, and to make me Chief-Justice at Ceylon, and they consented, and I went to Ceylon after mamma had been a year away ; and when I arrived at Ceylon I heard that my son had been almost dead, and that mamma was so ill that it was not likely she would ever come out to me, and I became very sorry : and I did not see anybody that I have ever known before. There was no John Bell, nor Lady Catherine, nor General Napier, nor Cecilia, nor Johnstone, nor Janet, nor the Butlers, nor any other body to comfort me or speak about mamma with, nor anybody except

Mr Selby and George that cared about me. I
felt very low-spirited and lonely, and like a tree
standing by itself that has lost all its leaves,
and I looked about for somebody that I thought
would not think it tiresome to hear about
mamma and you, and as I did not know anybody, or what sort of dispositions they had, I
was obliged to guess by their faces. I saw an
officer, who was tall and thin like Robert Baillie
of the 72d, and I thought that he looked of
an affectionate mild disposition, like dear Jimmy
Erskine, and Cousin Day, and Carolus Graham,
who are so fond of us, and that he would
let me speak to him about my wife and child
without thinking it tiresome, and that he would
let me love him and be kind to him like
Jimmy and the other cousins, although he was
no relation. So one day I took him a drive
into the country with me. I had been so
long living by myself without having prayers
every morning at breakfast-time and on Sunday
evenings, that I had fallen away a great deal
from the love and fear of God, and God had left
me to myself in a great measure, because I
had neglected His Word and become careless.
But God had not turned away His face altogether, but only hid it, neither had He forgotten
or forsaken me, because you know it is written,

'A woman may forget her sucking child, yet will I not forget thee, saith the Lord'; and also, 'I will never leave thee nor forsake thee.' So I had become careless in my speech, and used bad words thoughtlessly, that I had got into the habit of using when I was a young man and frequented gay company, and I spoke foolish things for want of something to say."

This picture, drawn by his own hand, of so important a member of society in the busy and prosperous colony, the chief law officer of the Crown, casting his eyes about with a remnant of the shyness of his Scotch youth, to see what face among the new society around looked kind enough to be made a confidant of, and who there was who would listen to his anxious talk about his wife and child without finding it tiresome, is most engaging and attractive. All did not go well, however, in this first drive. One wonders what the Chief-Justice said, with that grave young officer sitting by,—whether he launched too vigorous an epithet at an unwilling horse, or held in a too impetuous one with an objurgation, and what were the foolish things to which he gave utterance, before he ventured to open his heart as he desired, about his pretty young wife, who was far away, and little Laurence, who was the light of their eyes. The Officer—one feels it necessary to put his name with a capital, as if he had been in 'Sandford and Merton'—made no remark upon his eminent companion's freedom of speech; but when the Chief-Justice asked him to dinner some time later, declined, on the score that " by mixing in society I am acting inconsistently with my religious principles." This excuse awoke the slumbering conscience of Sir Anthony, who wrote again to the young soldier, asking if it was anything in him, in his conduct or conversation, which had occasioned the refusal, or if it was merely on general principles — in which latter case he hoped that they might still meet, as people of similar minds, in their evening rides or drives, and that if the absent wife was ever able to join him, she as well as he might have the advantage of the pious youth's society. This elicited a letter full of feeling from the young soldier, and a warm friendship was formed.

The whole narrative breathes of a time gone by. I fear we should be disposed to think the Officer sanctimonious and a religious prig in these changed days. But the genuine humility and moral sensitiveness of the middle - aged lawyer, judge and autocrat in his own sphere, is exceedingly touching and beautiful. These are not exactly

the qualities we look for in a Chief-Justice, any
more than the shy outlook for a sympathetic face.
He was so much impressed by the incident altogether that he reported it thus at great length
to his child, in the hope that when his Lowry was
as big as the Officer in question " he will do exactly as he did." " When I am better acquainted
with him I shall ask him, that in case I should die
soon, and he is ever near my son, to go to him,
and ask him if he ever associates with people
from whom he can learn anything bad, and to
ask him to show him this letter, and if he acts
upon it. And my Lowry must keep this letter
which I now write, and read it always on his
birthday ; and if he is able to draw all the morals
from it that it contains, and to act as Mr B. did,
if he never meets Mr B. on earth, he will be happy
with him in heaven. And I write this for my
son's welfare, and that mamma may know that
there is somebody here who will love and take
care of papa when she is far away." The Chief-
Justice of Ceylon is a little confused in style,
though that arose no doubt from writing down
to his correspondent of ten, and his appearance
here is not what we should expect from his
imposing position and authority : but how delightful is the glimpse of him thus afforded !
Chief-justices, after all, are but men ; they

yearn for wife and child like the humblest
individual, and are subject to the influence of
human approbation or disapproval.   But few,
very few, are those who would admit or yield
to the tacit reproof of a stranger with such
a tender conscience and so much humility.   I
fear his son would have been disposed to laugh
at the Officer and his grave young face.

The mother and child, thus so far separated
from the tender and longing head of the house,
spent some part of their time coming and going
at Condie, the ancestral home—"sweet Condie,"
as little Lowry called it—the old Scotch mansion-
house of which he spoke in after and graver
years.   There is a pretty anecdote of his childhood here, which seems to point at even an
earlier age than that mature ten years which he
possessed when his father wrote the letter above
quoted.   Certain ladies of the neighbourhood,
coming to call upon the laird's sister - in - law,
young Mrs Anthony from the Cape, were introduced into the drawing-room, where there seemed
to be nobody, but where the small boy was playing with his box of bricks in a corner.   Perhaps
the visitors did not perceive him ; perhaps thought
him too young to note what they were saying,
which was an imprudent confidence.   At all
events, they began to talk of the lady they were

waiting to see—what a pretty young woman she was, and what a pity the child should be so plain. At this point they were startled by the sudden uplifting of a small voice from the corner. "Ah," said the boy, moved, yet philosophically, impartially, by the criticism upon himself, "but I have very expressive eyes." The sense of humour, which never deserted him, must thus have shown itself at a very early period.

There is not very much appearance of it, however, in the schoolboy letters which he wrote from Mr Parr's school at Durnford Manor, near Salisbury, where he began his education. They are amusing sometimes, as every child's letters are, with their jumble of subjects and transparent innocent self-absorption; but it is happily evident that little Lowry, though something of a hothouse plant, brought up at his mother's feet, had none of the precocious development common to children accustomed to the constant society of their elders. The little letters are often accompanied by a note from the lady of the house, apologetic of poor Lowry's carelessness, or his handwriting, or the difficulty there was in getting him to write. On one occasion he loses his mother's letter before he has finished reading it, and begs her in the next to put down "some of the most importinate facts" of the lost epistle.

His style certainly lacks clearness. "All together," he says, "I am third in my class.
Græme, Alfred Montague, a queer little beggar,
who sends his complemences to you, but a nice
little chap upon the whole, he was sitting next
and rubbed it all out, till Mr Waring told him
to go away." On another occasion he begs his
dear mamma to let him send his letter on Tuesday, because it is more convenient, and because
Alfred Montague sends his on Tuesday. He
counts the weeks till the holidays, yet thinks
on the whole the time passes very quickly. "We
generally have what we call larks at night," says
the candid little boy. "There are two boys that
are very passionate, and we like, of course, to
tease them. We shut them up in the fives-
court, and they got in such what the boys call
a wax, which means a rage." "Do excuse my
both bad writing, and am not inclined for writing," he adds. In another Lowry falls a little
into the vein of religious retrospection in which
he has been trained. "You asked me to speak
to you as I used to do," he says; "I should tell
you some more of my besetting sins. One of
them is my not saying my prayers as I ought,
hurrying over them to get up in the morning
because I am late, and at night because it is
cold; another is my hiding what I do naughty

and keeping it from Mr Parr's eyes, not thinking the eye of God is upon me, a greater eye than man's; and another my cribing things from other boys, which is another word for stealing — not exactly stealing, but leads to it." After this calm discrimination of morals, he goes on to other matters. "I am such a horrid sumer" (sum-er—*i.e.*, arithmetician), he says, with felicitous vexation; "it is that that gets me down in my class so much. I was perfectly beaten last week, for they brought me down from top to bottom." There are many people who will feel the deepest sympathy with Lowry in his tribulations as a "horrid sumer." "Excuse the blots," he adds; "but I put it in my shelf, and when I came to get it to finish it, and it was out on the table—but I must now finish, for I am impatient." It cannot be said that the writing is much to Lowry's credit, and the anxious excuses of his master's wife are not without justification. But it is very touching to find these little letters so carefully preserved after fifty long years, so living in their childish freedom and confusion of over-active thought. The little fellow was not clever, so far as appeared; but he was the light of his mother's eyes, and already a favourite everywhere,—the brightest restless child, always doing, forming

already his succinct little opinions upon things
and men.

In 1841, Lady Oliphant—who during this interval had been spending her time partly in
England, partly in Scotland : at the paternal
house of Condie, which was paradise to Lowry
in the holidays ; at Wimbledon, in the house of
Major Oliphant,[1] another brother of her husband,
where the boy found comrades and companions
of an age similar to his own ; and for a considerable period in Edinburgh—joined Sir Anthony in
Ceylon. But it soon became apparent that to
be separated thus from her only child was too
great a strain upon the happiness and health of
the tender mother ; and she had not been long
settled in the island before imperative orders
were sent home for the return of Lowry, accompanied by a tutor who could carry on his education. "Send out the kid at once" was, I have
been told, the telegraphic summons ; but this
must be a fond invention of later days, for there
was then no telegraph, nor was Sir Anthony
at all likely to use such an expression. This
decision was simplified by the fact that there
were two boys, the sons of Mr Moydart, a

---

[1] Afterwards Lieutenant-Colonel James Oliphant, for many years
a director of the East India Company, and chairman of that body
in 1854.

neighbour at Colombo, of an age to share his lessons, and afford boyish company for the Chief-Justice's only child. Laurence, who had followed his schoolmaster, Mr Parr, to Preston, in Lancashire, where that gentleman had accepted a living, was summoned from school in all haste, and the much-trusted Uncle James at Wimbledon was charged with the choice of the tutor. The gentleman selected by Major Oliphant was Mr Gepp, now vicar of Higher Easton, near Chelmsford, a very young man just from Oxford, to whom, as to his pupil, the long journey overland, then a new route, and captivating to the imagination, was a great frolic and delight.

By this time Lowry had developed out of the early stage of childhood into an active and lively boy, eager for new experiences, and all the novelty and movement that were to be had. One bustling delightful visit he had at Condie to celebrate the marriage of his uncle, where there were tenants' dinners and outdoor dances, at which Lowry " kissed the lassies " with whom he danced, in delightful emulation of another young and gay uncle. He was between twelve and thirteen, with all his faculties awake, and his whole being agog for novelty and incident, when he set out to join his parents in the late winter of 1841. He has himself given an account of this, the first great journey which he made independently, the first he could fully recollect. It is astonishing to note the enormous difference between the means of travelling then and now, although the modern age of rapid movement had set in, and the English world was already exceedingly proud of itself for its first steps towards speed and ease in that long journey, the most important and momentous of all to Englishmen. From Boulogne, "where we arrived in a steamer direct from London Bridge"—to Marseilles occupied eight days and five nights of incessant diligence travel, varied by the incident of sticking in the snow at Chalons, from which they had to be dug out. The mail train rattles across the Continent from Calais to Brindisi now in three days. Yet I suspect Laurence and his companion had the best of it. Packed up in the *banquette* of the old-fashioned diligence, they saw and enjoyed everything,—the new unfamiliar landscape, the quaint villages, the old towns, the winterly brightness of France, newer and more original to them than anything is now to eyes so accustomed to discount every novelty as ours are. And the jolting, dirt, and wretchedness of the most highly organised *train de luxe*, with its sleeping-carriages and dining-saloons, one more odious than the other, yet the last word of luxurious organisation and supposed comfort in travelling — are a poor exchange for the more leisurely progress, which at least permitted a tranquil meal now and then, and unfolded the country through which he passed, and many amusing and agreeable incidents to the traveller.

"Adventures," somebody says, "come to the adventurous," and this first voyage of the boy who had so many before him was signalised by a visit, made necessary by an accident, to Mocha, a place very little visited either then or now by the Giaour, and where the Shereef was exceedingly civil to the English travellers—a civility, I believe, explained by the fact that an English gunboat lay not far off, though the strangers were unaware of this strong inducement to politeness on the part of their entertainers. The voyage altogether, with the repeated breakdowns of the ship and pauses for repairs (there was then no P. & O.), lasted about three months. We are not told to what pitch of despairing anxiety the parents in Ceylon had been driven by all this delay. But at last it came to an end, and Lowry settled down in the new brilliant Eastern world, where everything was a wonder, to his lessons with Mr Gepp and the Moydart boys, and to that close companionship with his mother which occu-

pied so large a portion of his life. She was still
a young woman—"there were but eighteen years
between us," he used to say; and though Lady
Oliphant loved to be obeyed, yet she had from
his infancy placed the boy—the "Darling," as his
father invariably calls him, with a little affectionate mockery—in a position of influence and equality not perhaps very safe for a child, but always
delightful between these two; for the quick-
witted and sharp - sighted boy had always a
chivalrous tenderness for his mother, even when,
as happened sometimes, he found it necessary to
keep her in her proper place. I have been told
an amusing little illustration of this in an incident that happened one morning when, the
tutor's scheme of work appearing unsatisfactory
to Lady Oliphant, she came into the schoolroom
to announce her desire that it should be altered.
To do this before the open-eyed and all-observant
boys was, perhaps, not very judicious, and the
young preceptor was wounded and vexed. There
was probably a sirocco, or its equivalent, blowing
—that universal excuse for every fault of temper
in warm latitudes—and a quarrel was imminent,
when Lowry rose from his books and came to the
rescue. "Mamma, this is not the right place for
you," said the heaven-born *diplomat*, offering her
his arm, with the fine manners which no doubt

she had been at such pains to teach him, and leading her away—no doubt half amused, half pleased, although half angry, with the social skill of the boy.

An education thus conducted, and subject to all the social interruptions of the lively colonial life, where visitors were continually coming and going, and the house of the Chief-Justice a centre of entertainment and pleasant friendliness, must have had its drawbacks. But except for the short period at Salisbury and Preston when he was a little boy, Laurence never was subjected to educational discipline of a severe kind. He was one of the pupils of Life, educated mainly by what his keen eyes saw and his quick ears heard, and his clear understanding and lively wit picked up, amid human intercourse of all kinds. He was in no way the creation of school or college. When, as happens now and then, an education so desultory, so little consecutive or steady as his, produces a brilliant man or woman, we are apt to think that the accidental system must be on the whole the best, and education a delusion, like so many other cherished things; but the conclusion is a rash one, and it is perhaps safest in this, as in so many other directions, to follow the beaten way. I do not think he himself ever regretted it, and he had little or none of the traditionary respect for university training which is so general. He had a most cheerful delightful life, between the gay little capital Colombo—where he knew everybody, and saw everything that occurred, and took his share in entertaining great officials, governors and suchlike, on their way to and from India, as well as less important crowds, civil and military—and that home of health, Newera Ellia, among the hills, which the Oliphants were among the first to make popular. In after days a continual flight of letters, daily recording everything that happened, went up to that green and wholesome spot from the young man of much business in the court at Colombo and elsewhere, to his mother; but in the meantime Lowry accompanied her in all her moves, and the strong bond of united life, so possible, so perfect, between an intelligent child and a woman full of simplicity, notwithstanding her intelligence and maturity, grew stronger day by day.

CHAPTER II.

BEGINNING LIFE.

IT was not, however, so much the intention of his parents, who were fully purposed to complete their son's education in the usual way, as accident, which secured to Laurence the exemption from ordinary studies and restraints, which conduced so much to make him what he was. He had been sent home again to the care of a tutor in England, about whom I have not been able to obtain any information, and was being prepared for the university and the ordinary course of a young Englishman's training, when his father returned to England from Ceylon with a two years' leave of absence—the first real holiday which probably the hardworking Judge had ever had. " I was on the point of going up to Cambridge at the time," says Laurence, in his ' Episodes from a Life of Adventure ' ; " but when he announced that he intended to travel for a couple of years

with my mother on the Continent, I represented
so strongly the superior advantages, from an
educational point of view, of European travel
over ordinary scholastic training, and my arguments were so urgently backed by my mother,
that I found myself, to my great delight, transferred from the quiet of a Warwickshire vicarage
to the Champs Elysées in Paris ; and, after passing the winter there, spent the following year
roaming over Germany, Switzerland, and the
Tyrol." It was in the year 1846 that this trans-
formation was effected, and the boy turned once
for all into the " rolling stone " which he continued to be for all the rest of his life. There
could be no more exciting period for a plunge
into the Continent, which was so entirely new to
the little party of travellers—as novel and strange
as if they had been rustics newly setting out from
their fields—notwithstanding their acquaintance
with the Eastern world and places far away. " I
often wondered, while thus engaged," he continues, " whether I was not more usefully and
instructively employed than labouring painfully
over the differential calculus; and whether the execrable *patois* of the peasants in the Italian valleys,
which I took great pains in acquiring, was not
likely to be of quite as much use to me in after-
life as ancient Greek." This is a question which

it is never very easy to answer. If it were put in another form, and we were to ask whether the brilliant and remarkable individuality of Laurence Oliphant were not worth a host of ordinary university men trimmed to one pattern, it would be simple enough; yet we may be permitted to believe that the ancient Greek and the profounder culture might have saved him and the world from some wild dreams of after-life, without diminishing the originality and force of his being. These, however, are speculations without use; for no doubt the manner of development is all involved in the product, and no man can contradict his nature. However, this free life and acquaintance in the dawn of individual intelligence with the ways of thinking and life of other nations, had doubtless much to do in determining his career.

In 1847, the family party, ensconced in the comfortable ark used in old days by such leisurely travellers, with its varying team of four or six horses, according as it climbed or descended the mountain road, passed across the Alps to Italy, then seething with a universal fever of revolution. There never was such ideal travelling as in this lurching, heavy, altogether delightful vehicle, packed in a hundred pockets with everything one could want, pausing wherever it seemed good to the voyager, and with a long rest in the heat of the day at some delightful old town or picturesque village. The travellers thus gained a knowledge of the country in detail—its endless stores of beauty, its ever-friendly people, its humble shrines and fortresses, its overflowing life, such as no hurried railway can afford. One can travel all over Italy now without hearing a word of anything but formal Italian, the language of the books; no need to puzzle what the peasants say, though it is often so quaint and witty. But it was otherwise in those days. No doubt Lowry occupied the covered *banquette* in front, from which he could give notice of every new *castello* or change in the prospect. He was seventeen, at the age when enjoyment of this kind is unalloyed, and the air and movement and constant change are a pure delight. And at such a crisis there was much for an intelligent boy to see and do. The enthusiasm which was growing and swelling through the entire country went to his young head, easily touched at all times by the contagion of popular excitement. He recounts the "salient features" of this wonderful journey as "indelibly stamped upon my memory."

"I shall never forget joining a roaring mob one evening, bent I knew not upon what errand, and getting forced by the pressure of the crowd, and my own eagerness, into the front rank, just as we

reached the Austrian Legation, and seeing the
ladders passed to the front, and placed against
the wall, and the arms torn down : then I remember, rather from love of excitement than
any strong political sympathy, taking hold, with
hundreds of others, of the ropes which were attached to them, and dragging them in triumph to
the Piazza del Popolo, where a certain Ciceroac-
chio, who was a great tribune of the people in
those days, and a wood-merchant, had a couple of
carts loaded with wood standing ready ; and I remember their contents being tumultuously upset,
and heaped into a pile, and the Austrian arms
being dragged on the top of them, and a lady—
I think the Princess Pamphili Doria, who was
passing in a carriage at the time—being compelled to descend, and being handed a flaming
torch, with which she was requested to light the
bonfire, which blazed up amid the frantic demon-
strations of delight of a yelling crowd, who formed
round it a huge ring, joining hands, dancing and
capering like demons,—in all of which I took an
active part, getting home utterly exhausted, and
feeling that somehow or other I had deserved well
of my country.

" And I remember upon another occasion being
roused from my sleep, about one or two in the
morning, by the murmur of many voices, and look-

ing out of my window and seeing a dense crowd moving beneath, and rushing into my clothes and joining it—for even in those early days I had a certain moss-gathering instinct—and being borne along I knew not whither, and finding myself at last one of a shrieking, howling mob, at the doors of the Propaganda, against which heavy blows were being directed by improvised battering-rams; and I remember the doors crashing in, and the mob crashing after them, to find empty cells and deserted corridors, for the monks had sought safety in flight. And I remember standing on the steps of St Peter's while Pope Pio Nono gave his blessing to the volunteers that were leaving for Lombardy to fight against the Austrians, and seeing the tears roll down his cheeks—as I supposed, because he hated so much to have to do it. These are events which are calculated to leave a lasting impression on the youthful imagination."

One wonders rather how the excellent judge felt when he found his son thus rushing in where full-grown diplomatists feared to tread, compromising himself—if anybody had as yet minded which side Lowry took—even perhaps compromising England, had it been known that the young abettor of revolution was the son of a distinguished British official; or whether the mother did not suffer agonies of anxiety while the crowd rushed by with her boy, as she must have known, in the thick of the mischief, whatever it was. However, no harm would seem to have come of it, unless indeed this first taste of the sweetness of excitement and the fire of the multitude in motion awakened the latent spark in the mind of one destined to see so much of such movement in after-life.

At the end of this extraordinary " education by contact," the remarkable substitute for Cambridge which commended itself to the Oliphant family, Laurence returned with his father to Ceylon, where he seems to have been considered old enough at nineteen to enter into a quasi-public life as the Judge's secretary, and where he very soon advanced to the position of a barrister, pleading in the supreme courts, and conducting a great deal of very serious business. He had been engaged in " twenty-three murder cases," he himself tells us, before he had attained as many years of age. We find a rapid outline of his life at this period in the little notes which he dashed off daily from Colombo and other places to his mother at Newera Ellia, the hill-station which is to Ceylon what Simla is to India : sometimes written from court while the fate of some of his murderers hung in the balance, and he cries out indignant that had they been but tried by papa or before an

English jury they would have been safe; sometimes in the moment before dinner, when he is
preparing to entertain, in his mother's place,
papa's dinner-party of serious officials or distinguished strangers; sometimes from the cricket-
ground; sometimes after a ball. Lowry was
everywhere, in the centre of everything, affec-
tionately contemptuous of papa's powers of taking
care of himself, and laying down the law, in
delightful ease of love and unquestioned suprem-
acy, to his mother. There is not a sentence in
those little letters to quote, but they place the
position before us with the most vivid yet playful
clearness. Papa, we may infer, smiled a little
sardonically, with that sense of amusement in the
precautions taken for him, which is one of the
privileges of a parent; but the mother accepted
it all, with pride and confidence unbounded in her
boy, to whom it is evident, though he took such
care of everybody, a great deal of freedom was
permitted. His shooting expeditions, in which
he sometimes ran considerable risk, for the game
in Ceylon is big and dangerous, were reproduced
long afterwards in sketches so brilliant and life-
like that it is easy to see how he must have
thrown himself into those exciting moments of
life in the jungle—though papa was left to take
care of himself at such periods in the distant

assizes in different parts of the island, whence
his son had escaped to more exciting experiences.
One does not know whether any recollection of
this bright-faced lad, with his boundless high
spirits and energy, still lingers in Ceylon ; but the
whole island comes to view in his letters, in rapid
life-giving touches, a sort of dissolving panorama
of a busy society in colonial completeness, great
and small, with its eager interests and the buzz
of the hundred little intrigues, arrangements, dis-
agreements, all of such absorbing interest, all so
entirely dead and gone. The Governor's house
at Newera Ellia still bears the name, we believe,
of the Oliphants, and the island is governed from
the spot where Laurence's mother waited for her
daily courier, and saw through Lowry's letters, as
in a camera, everything that was being done.

This period of home-dwelling, however, did not
last very long. In the end of the year 1850,
Laurence being then twenty-one, an unusual and
interesting visitor touched at Ceylon on his way
from England back to India. He was one of the
first native envoys ever sent from the unknown
East, and his appearance had been hailed in England with a warmth of curiosity and interest which
was fresh in these days, when public curiosity
had not degenerated into the foolish and selfish
society fever over a novelty, which makes social

success nowadays so little of a compliment. Jung Bahadour was a revelation to the country, which jumped at the idea, not unnatural in the then ignorance of Eastern affairs, and always delightful, that India was about to accept with enthusiasm the culture and sentiments of the West, and that this enlightened and splendid native prince, with his blazing diamonds and his advanced views, was but the first of a noble harvest of liberal minds and civilising measures to come. It is to be supposed that he must have produced a similar impression at Ceylon, notwithstanding the more complete knowledge and the small public faith in " natives " with which a colonial community is endowed. At all events, the romance about him, the distance and novelty of his unknown country far away, and the instinct of the traveller and adventurer which was so strong in young Laurence, combined to surround the envoy with a halo of attraction. It seems wonderful that an only child, so cherished and adored, should have been able to persuade his parents to consent to such a wild expedition. But they would seem at all times to have had the most unbounded confidence in him, and conviction that his impulses were not to be restrained, nor his conduct made the subject of parental dictation.

It is very probable that their friends con-
demned Sir Anthony and his wife for their fond
submission and concurrence in all Lowry's vagaries, as no doubt they censured his want of
formal education and the irregularity of his
training. On this particular occasion one of
them at least seems to have spoken out. "My
approval of your retaining Lowry in Ceylon was
never meant to extend to such an excursion as
that which he has undertaken to Nepaul, which
can hardly improve his legal prospects, financi-
ally or professionally," says one of the most
trusted counsellors of the family. Another friend,
however, highly disapproves Lady Oliphant's desire to retain him by her side, and especially
that she should tell him his father approves
while she does not, thus raising a feeling of
conflict in his mind. "Let him alone," this
lady says. Thus it was evident that there were
debates on the question. But the young man's
wishes carried the day. He left Ceylon with
his new friend in December 1851. The result
of the expedition was a book, the first of many
vivid sketches of adventure, in which, as happened to him in his general good luck on more
than one occasion, he had an entirely new field to
explore. What is more important, however, for
our present purpose, is that it brings us his own

account of himself in a series of letters, carefully marked by his mother's hand No. 1, 2, &c., in which the story of his first adventure by himself in the world is told. The little narrative begins with a sketch of a fellow-passenger in the steamer in which he leaves Ceylon, whose character he conceives to be something like his own, for which idea it is worth while to quote it.

" He is a pleasant enough fellow as a companion, but abominably selfish and a thorough charlatan. His faults in the latter respect are something like mine—in fact, I saw that I might well take warning from him. His interest was the first thing which he considered, and he was rather unscrupulous in making everything subservient to it. He toadied me like fun, and thinks I don't see through him. But I must not be so dreadfully uncharitable, though I could not but be struck by the almost providential neighbourhood of a man who seemed myself exaggerated."

Laurence must have corrected early these faults, like the " besetting sin " of " cribing," of which he accuses himself on an earlier occasion. Certainly, self-interest was the last thing that his worst enemy could lay to his charge.

" The Minister " [Jung Bahadour], he adds,
" is a glorious fellow, and we are great friends.
He amused himself all day shooting at bottles.
I have seen him hit three running fastened to
the yard-arm ; first hitting the bottle with right
barrel, and then the neck, which was still hanging, with the left. He knows a little English,
but his stock is confined to making love—'Give
me a kiss,' and a few other phrases equally short
and sweet. We had great fun jumping, but I
beat his head off, whereat he was much dis-
quieted ; but being determined not to be done,
he immediately commenced hanging by his heels
in ropes in the most fantastic way, which I found
impossible, not having been, like him, shampooed
from earliest infancy. Oliphant Sahib being considered unpronounceable, I am Lowry Sahib, in
return for which I call the young colonel (brother
of Jung) Fe-fi-fo-fum Sahib, that being the near-
est approach I can make to his name."

Calcutta the young man found worth coming
to see, even if he were to go no farther, and was
much amused to find himself the fashion, and
sought after everywhere. " The idea of going
up to Nepaul with Jung Bahadour on a shooting
expedition is my passport everywhere, and con-
stitutes me a lion at once. Mrs Gordon takes

a delight in introducing me to all the big-wigs.
She certainly has a great knack of making one
feel satisfied with one's self, and would spoil the
most modest young man. So you must not mind
my giving myself airs when I come back, unless
somebody takes me down a peg in Nepaul. If
I were going to live in Calcutta," he adds, " I
should not devote myself to seeing and being
seen in the way I do now; but for a week I
think I ought to see as much of men and manners
here as possible. I hope you are not afraid of
the gaiety : it is but for a short time and of no
very serious nature, and I make a point of being
alone a good deal in the morning. I hope you
will write me a letter of good advice, as I want
it now, and certainly shall by the time I shall
get it; and never mind boring me—it won't at
all." Thus it will be seen the boy was still a
dutiful boy, thinking of his mother's anxieties,
and how much she feared that balls and other
vanities and perpetual society would be against
his spiritual advantage, notwithstanding the independence and freedom of his twenty-one years.

The mode of travelling, when at last he started
up country, was peculiar, but it seems to have
been comfortable enough. He and his companion
went from Calcutta to Benares in " a large coach
which only holds two, but in which two very

good beds can be made up. In this, which is very comfortable, Cavanagh and I have been living for the last two days, and shall have to do so for four more, making it our home both by day and night. Ten coolies drag us along a very good road. In the mornings and evenings we walk alongside or sit on the coach-box, and if we have a lazy team, drive them along in a most barbarous way. Papa would be amused at this specimen of Indian backwardness, being dragged for nearly five hundred miles along a magnificent road in a four-horse coach by men instead of horses the whole way. It would have delighted you, however," he adds, "for the coolies never shy, stumble, nor run away, or misbehave in any other way but being lazy and importunate."

On arriving at Benares he found himself in the midst of the bustle of preparation for the great hunting-party of which everybody was talking.

" Everybody says I am lucky to get such a chance of seeing sport, and fellows are making all sorts of interest with him [Jung] to be allowed to come too, and I daresay we shall make up a formidable party. The Jung is an immense lion among the native princes here, who all want to go home. He took up his caste (forfeited by his voyage) the day before yester-

day, so I missed the ceremony ; but it only consisted of all the party who had gone home (*i.e.*,
to England), taking a bath in the presence of
numbers of spectators. He has three hundred
men of the Nepaul army down here as an escort.
There are six hundred elephants waiting for us
at Sagaulee to beat the Terai, and if they don't
get something out of the jungle, it's a pity.
Look for Sagaulee on the map : it is on the Nepaul
frontier, and we begin our battue from there,
going some miles into the Nepaul country and
coming back to it previous to starting for Khatmandhu."

The account which he gives his mother of the
books he carried with him to occupy his moments
of leisure is added. " I think you will approve
of the selection,—Guizot's ' History of English
Revolution,' Bourrienne's ' Memoirs,' Lord Mahon's
' Life of Condé,' a Hindostanee dialogue — and
some of Sir A. Buller's small vols. of Paul de
Kock, which he has lent me." Let us hope Lady
Oliphant believed these last to be theological
treatises.

" The Jung is as civil and kind to me as ever,
and I am beginning to say a word or two to
him in Hindostanee now. The house abounds

in children, who make the most desperate noise in Hindostanee without the slightest control. To-night the Jung reviews his troops for the benefit of the General, and we are all going to see it, as they say it is a curious sight. He showed me his dogs to-day, also his falcons, so you may imagine me unhooding my bird as in the olden days."

The final scene of the hunting-party was only reached after various other detentions on the road among friends who sprang up upon the young man's path everywhere: old soldiers who had been at school with papa, younger ones who had got their cadetships from Uncle James, or who had married somebody's sister in one or other category, or who knew Perthshire and all the people there, or who had received the hospitality of Lady Oliphant at the Cape,—those contingencies which seem to happen so much more readily in India than anywhere else. Laurence makes special note of the young ladies, who were generally pretty, and always lively and delightful, and with whom he felt himself entitled to flirt with much vehemence, since a single evening was the limit of his intercourse with them. "I have taken to making love furiously, as I know I am going away immediately," is the unprincipled confession he makes ; and he begs his mother not to be afraid of his proceedings in this respect, which would seem to have been a weakness of hers. It was after a ball, and a tender leave-taking at two o'clock in the morning, that the young man flung himself into his palanquin and slept " far into the following day," while his bearers jogged along, carrying him to his destination.

" We found the Jung encamped in a picturesque spot. The scene altogether was very enlivening : four thousand men, with elephants, horses, camels, bivouacking in a large mango-grove, with our hut pitched near the Jung's, who, when we arrived, was out shooting. We soon joined him on a gorgeously attired elephant provided for our use, and found him on a still more handsomely got - up one, his brothers on another. But I must tell you about his little bride, who was with him, a pretty little girl of thirteen or fourteen, almost as fair as a European, and as he calls her ' My beautiful missis.' She is the daughter of the Coorg Rajah, and was betrothed to Jung in Benares. He seems very fond of her, and kind to her, and she looks very happy. I like him more and more. He is so thoroughly European. To give you an instance of it. One day, while calling on him, the Rajah of

Bhurtpore was announced, so his guard turned out, and the gentleman was received by Jung, and led to a couch with due honour, when after a complimentary speech on both sides, Jung said to him, 'Your Highness must excuse me, as I have important business with these gentlemen,' pointing to us, therewith coolly leading the Rajah with equal state to the door. He came back a moment after, laughing and rubbing his hands, saying, 'That's the way to get over an interview with one of these natives.' Of course he had no business whatever with us. He is making his little betrothed shake hands, and behave otherwise quite like a European lady, and instead of shutting her up, she always goes about with him. We march ten miles a-day, starting out at a quick march with his troops and band, which is a very large one and plays English tunes. The Jung always takes his gun with him, and shoots every cockyolly bird he comes across. You may imagine, therefore, how much I am enjoying myself. The game consists of quails, hares, and partridges. The Jung sends us our dinner, which consists of rice boiled with ghee, and eighteen or twenty other condiments, served in leaves and scented, so that one feels as if one were eating greasy smells. We have consequently come to the determination of accepting

Jung's dinner, but of providing ourselves with
something edible as well as odoriferous. The
chutney smells exactly like the young colonel;
it is a very nice smell, but one does not like it
to get further than one's nose. I have found
out the philosophy of travelling. In travelling
you are much more likely to have excitement of
one sort or another than leading a humdrum
life; but as happiness consists in anticipation,
all you have to do is continually to anticipate
excitement and you will always be happy, whereas in the other case excitement is so very unlikely that you can't work yourself up to the
anticipation of it. Then there is intense enjoyment in eating even ghee and smells when
you have gone twenty-four hours without eating
anything, also in sleeping when you have been
two nights awake — all pleasures to which you
are a stranger."

After this there comes a sudden digression,
caused by the happy accident of falling into
a great picnic party which was spending a few
days in tents at no great distance from the
"Jung's" encampment—of all the amusements
of which young Laurence and his companion
were made free, and which suggests the startling question in his next letter, "How would

you like a Roman Catholic daughter-in-law?"
I have already said that young ladies were
much in the thoughts of this traveller of
twenty-one, and he had already intimated with
much delight that he alone could "polk" of
the assembled party, and therefore had it all
his own way. He enlarges for a page of this
letter upon the particular lady in question,
who was not only very pretty but very sensible,
clever, and lady-like, and would not be flirted
with at any price, which, adds this experienced
youth, "made it so dangerous. I began by trying for fun to cut out two fellows who were
rivals, and I succeeded so triumphantly that it
became nearly earnest, to the disgust of one, who
cut me dead at last; but we made it up when we
killed the tiger yesterday. If you knew how
much I am envied you would excuse my conceit,
which is becoming unbearable." It is perhaps
the reaction from this delightful sensation of
triumph that makes him a little discontented
with his real host, the Jung, when he rejoins the
camp.

"The Jung has not behaved well to us in
the shooting line, and we are rather cool with
him on that account. He makes arrangements
for us to go out with him, but being a very

jealous sportsman, has contrived twice to give
us the slip with his elephants," which leads the
young men to the resolution of setting off on
horseback by themselves to Khatmandhu and
abandoning the party. "Travelling in India,"
Laurence adds, "is totally different from travelling in any other country. The comfort and
pleasure of being made at home in a nice house
with nice people, instead of going to an inn, is
not to be told. By so doing one is per-
petually thrown with new people, who have to
be learnt—as is also the knack of making yourself agreeable in the shortest possible time.
There are certain hobbies and subjects which
every one has in India, and in which I am becoming perfect, having of course no particular
opinion on them myself, 'but what master likes.'
Then the change of climate and scene puts one
in good health and spirits, and the numerous
little trials of temper that one undergoes tend
to make one a philosopher. I rarely get further
than looking a little sulky now and then at a
man whose neck I should like to wring slowly.
The Nepaulese are excessively stupid, and hor-
ribly good-humoured, so I can't do anything else
with them ; but the Hindostanees are sulky and
alive to ridicule, so I get on very well with bullying them jocosely. . . . The next best thing to

having repose of mind is looking as if you had it, and I often wish I had a pleasant expression of countenance in my pocket, which I could fasten on my face when wanted."

This letter—which is tinged with a certain shade of discontent, with an "I am not so full of the young lady" at the end—after a few days' interval is however reopened in great excitement to narrate "the most magnificent day's sport I ever had in my life."

"We started early this morning elephant-catching, but did not come up with the herd till two o'clock. I insisted upon going, much against the Minister's [Jung's] wish, who said it was impossible for me to do it : however, saying he was no longer responsible, he gave me an elephant on which was nothing but a sack of straw lashed firmly on, with a loop of rope to hold by. Taking off cap and shoes, I was told to stick to this through thick and thin, throwing myself off the elephant when passing under branches, and holding on with my hands to swing myself on him again. Two regiments with a lot of elephants had been sent to beat the jungle ; and when the herd appeared, about a hundred more, on one of which I was, started in full pursuit. Besides holding on, I had to thrash the elephant with a spiked piece of wood : you may imagine it was no joke, seeing a bough before you which grazed your hands and arms passing, not six inches above the elephant's back, the mahout doing likewise. It was certainly the most violent exertion I ever underwent, and once the elephant came down a tremendous trip on his nose, which nearly dislocated every bone in my body. On we rushed, regardless of everything. A pack of a hundred elephants in full cry is a curious sight, with two nearly naked men on each, swaying about like bolsters, now on one side, now on the other, or slipping down to the root of the tail and holding on by the crupper. We got two (wild) elephants separated, and followed them close, when suddenly I was enveloped in smoke, and very much astonished by a dozen or more guns let off in my face. The elephants had doubled back, and this was a salvo from a lot of soldiers hidden in the grass, who immediately afterwards threw away their guns and made for the trees. But the elephants were so bewildered by the smoke and hot pursuit, that they kept on until they thought it time to turn and charge, which they did, but took nothing by their motion, our elephants standing like rocks, while the others were belabouring their sides and backs with their trunks. Finding there was no help for it, they tried to bolt; but that was not so easy, each of them, in the meantime, having had two nooses thrown round their necks, which four elephants were all pulling different ways. They were two mothers with two little ones, and the poor little things got dreadfully jostled, and roared vehemently upon being separated from their mothers. I am the only European that has ever attempted to follow, and Sir Henry Lawrence is the only one that has even seen anything of one from a distance, and the Jung says that was nothing to this. He would call me a brick if he had a Nepaulese word for it. You need not be afraid of my going out again; there is not the slightest chance of it, as we leave the elephant country the first thing in the morning."

After this high point of excitement the narrative drops to lower levels. At Khatmandhu, when the travellers reached it at last, things were not so well with the Jung as had been hoped, and Laurence and his companion, though with much reluctance, released him from a promise he had made to allow them to explore the country—a privilege never yet granted to any European, and likely to do the Minister harm if he permitted it. "He finds his position here anything but satisfac-

tory; the Durbar look suspiciously upon him, as
being a friend of England, an idea which many
little circumstances have tended to confirm; so
the Jung's head is not likely to remain long on
his shoulders, notwithstanding the cool way he
orders everybody about, from the king downwards. This we remarked at Durbar yesterday,
when he had his most devoted followers close behind his chair with double-barrelled rifles (loaded),
while the men he was afraid of were just in front
of him." The excitement of the journey was
thus cut short, as well as the young travellers'
hopes of exploring an altogether new country,
and having really something worth writing about.
Nothing remained for it, accordingly, but to push
on along the beaten ways, and join Lord Gros-
venor's party, which had been circling Laurence's
line of voyage for some time without ever coming
to an encounter. It is needless to follow him in
his detailed journeys, or even in the mixture of
diffidence and self-confidence with which he drives
up " with a carriage full of luggage " to the house
of a stranger to whom he has no tie except a
letter of introduction in his pocket, thinking it
"an unparalleled piece of impudence," yet consoled by the thought that " it is the custom in
India ": no need to say that he is always received with open arms.

There are, however, some bits of more serious thought in these letters, and occasionally scraps of self-analysis, called forth evidently by the pious mother's questions anent her boy's spiritual state. It is difficult, he says, to practise habits of self-examination riding upon an elephant, with a companion who is always talking or singing within a few feet; but it is otherwise in a palkee, which "is certainly a dull means of conveyance," but "forces one into one's self more than anything." The result of Laurence's self-ponderings is, that he discerns his great weakness to be "flexibility of conscience, joined to a power of adapting myself to the society into which I may happen to be thrown."

"It originated, I think, in a wish to be civil to everybody, and a regard for people's feelings, and has degenerated into a selfish habit of being agreeable to them, simply to suit my own convenience. I think I can be firm enough when I have an object to gain, and have not even the excuse of being so easily led as I used to think. I am only led when it is to pay, which is a most sordid motive—in fact, the more I see of my own character, the more despicable it appears, a being so deeply hypocritical that I can hardly trust myself; hence arose a disinclination ever to speak about myself. How blind one is to one's own interest not to see that, putting it on one's own ground, it would pay much better to be an upright God-fearing man than anything else! Fortunately religion is a thing that one cannot acquire from such a motive, or I am sure I should have done so before this."

No doubt that their son should make such a confession, or any confession breathing of self-dissatisfaction, would be agreeable to the parents— to the Judge, who had spoken naughty words and been so sorry for them, and to the anxious religious mother, always longing after his spiritual advantage. But perhaps Laurence felt that he had been a little hard upon himself. He ends by hoping "there is no humbug in it. It is honest as far as I know, but *don't believe in it implicitly*," he says; while in another letter he shows himself disposed to defend the "flexibility" of which he had just accused his own character and conscience. He is aware of "having Ferentcz's [an uncle] knack of making myself agreeable," but thinks it is to a great extent without any harm in it.

"If an old general likes to hear himself speak, why should you not look interested, however bored you may feel? why should you not take an interest in poor Mrs So-and-so, who has gone wrong, or been beaten by her husband, if Mrs General does? I got a tiffin out of an old couple at Benares simply in that way, and C. says, ' Why, I never saw such a fellow as you, Oliphant ; you are a favourite everywhere im- mediately.' I do not give myself any credit for it, mind ; on the contrary, nothing is easier, and I inherit it from your side of the house evidently. But the tendency I see to be bad in fact."

One may perhaps be inclined to wish that this tendency, to be agreeable and sympathetic, and to look interested even when you are bored, were a little more general ; but it is curious to find that a man, specially distinguished for tak- ing his own independent way in life, and that a most individual, not to say eccentric, one, should have been alarmed by his own early inclination to be all things to all men—a delightful faculty, however, which he retained, in the midst of a life more unfettered by other people's opinions or by any conventional rule than almost any other of his generation, to the very end.

There is nothing more charming in these youthful letters than the cordial and genuine response of this spoiled child to the affection lavished upon him. His mother's advices are not

only received well, but asked for with a sincerity
that cannot be doubted—a very unusual trait in
a young man of twenty-one; and the chance
references to his father, still papa to the home-
loving young adventurer, are always delightful.
Had papa but been there, he and Lowry would
have waited for no escort, feared no harm, but
set off lightly on foot through the prohibited
Nepaul. There is no such travelling companion,
the young man says, as papa. The men of his
own age are as nice fellows as can be, whom he
delights to emulate in every bodily exercise, to win
a genial triumph over either in the elephant-hunt
or the new polka, making a friendship for life
even out of a ball-room rivalry; but, after all,
there is nobody like his father for real companionship. Nor is there anybody so acute as
the Judge in appreciation of character,—a power
of which so many people are destitute, but which
Lowry modestly concludes he has himself inherited, as he has inherited the knack of pleasing
people from his mother's side of the house. His
eagerness to get home, to have post-horses ordered for him on the Kandy road, to lose not
a moment in reaching his mother's side, shows
how little the adoration of that home had spoiled
him. Thus ended the young man's first essay
of independent life,—a sufficiently wild flight to

be the first, and a most characteristic one. He had been filling the position of private secretary to his father since the return of the family from Europe three years before, at, he somewhere says, the exceedingly liberal salary of £400 a-year. And it was on his savings that he accomplished the rapid and brilliant rush through India which was the beginning both of his life of adventure and of his literary career.

CHAPTER III.

THE BAR—THE EXPEDITION TO RUSSIA.

It was perhaps scarcely possible that after such a taste of freedom, and of the social life for which he was so admirably constituted, the young man should settle down again at Ceylon to his irregular bar practice and existence of official routine. He had already felt the difficulty of being called upon to plead "before papa," which lessened his sphere, and he was also aware that his knowledge of law was imperfect for one who intended to adopt that profession (which, besides, he hated). Accordingly but a few months elapsed before his mind was finally made up to quit Ceylon, and try his fortune in the greater world. The time was approaching at which Sir Anthony would be able to resign his appointment, and retire from public work, and it was decided that Lady Oliphant should accompany her son home, *en attendant* the happy period fixed for the Judge's retirement ; for

it was evidently felt to be inexpedient that Laurence should lose any more time in qualifying himself for the more serious work of life.   Perhaps
some parental, or rather maternal, anxiety about
the health of the beloved boy had been alleged
to friends as a reason for this step, for I find a
letter to Sir Anthony from a friend in Gibraltar
who goes out to the steamer to greet the travellers in passing, and who announces that "Lowry
looked anything but delicate.   I should judge
him a great, stout, eleven-stone fellow, able to
give me a thoroughly good thrashing on an emergency."   Stout, in the sense which the word
generally bears, he never was, but well knit,
active, and muscular, with that promptitude of
eye and observation which are the most admirable
of additions to strength and courage.   His own
letters to his father left behind in Ceylon are
admirable, full of playfulness and graphic description, a little more free and less serious than those
to his mother, dashed off with a flying pen, and
full at first of all the humours of the little sea-
society on board ship, which always lend themselves to the remarks of the social critic.   The
mother and son arrived in England in the
end · of October 1851, finding the gloomy sea
in the Channel "easily recognisable from its
John Bull appearance," and already "luxuriat-

ing in English fog and damp." Although he knew very little of his own country, London was full of friends, and before he had been more than a month or two in England, he had resumed a hundred old friendships and made as many new ones, among his father's old companions and the men of his own generation. He decided to enter at Lincoln's Inn, where various people assured him he might be called to the Bar very speedily in consideration of his previous studies and practical experience in Ceylon. In those days it was not a matter of strict examination as it is now, and to have read for a year with a barrister was sufficient qualification. Certainly Laurence, with his social tastes and the habit of succeeding without severe preliminary labour, was the last man in the world for the ordeal of examinations, to which probably he would not have submitted, and certainly would not have "crammed" for. There is not much evidence indeed from first to last that he was greatly in earnest about this study. "I think," he says, "if I get up the two or three books necessary for acquiring a proper knowledge of mercantile law, including bills of exchange, together with the law of evidence, pleading and real property may take care of themselves." The beginning of that other most curious but most wonderful branch of legal study, which consists of eating dinners, is however more amusing. He describes it to his father in an early letter, so that it is evident he had lost no time in entering upon this severe portion of his education.

"LONDON, *Nov.* 24, 1851.

"I have eaten some stringy boiled beef at Lincoln's Inn Hall in company with three hundred others, not one soul of whom I had ever seen before; but I unhesitatingly talked to my next neighbour, and soon, by dropping in an unconcerned manner remarks upon a tiger I knocked over here, and a man I defended for murder there, talking learnedly about Ceylon affairs, &c., &c., incited the curiosity of those whose reserve would not otherwise have allowed them to notice me, too much to let them remain silent. Still I felt rather verdant on first entering, and was only saved from sitting down at the table appropriated to barristers by hearing one man remark he was not going to sit there, as So-and-so was his senior; so I concluded that if he was *his* senior he was most certainly mine, and choosing the youngest-looking man I could find, I seated myself next him."

The mother and son began their life in England in a cottage at East Sheen, lent to them by one

of their many friends, where they immediately
found themselves much at home among a number
of agreeable neighbours, including the family of
Sir Henry Taylor, the author of 'Philip van
Artevelde,' whom Laurence describes as the "idol
of the whole neighbourhood, made love to by the
entire female portion of the community." But a
young man with dinners to eat in Lincoln's Inn,
and many other engagements on hand, soon discovered that to be so far out of town was incon-
venient, and indeed impossible. It is with great
gravity and conviction that he states his preference for England, meaning London, a little later.

"The longer I stay in England, the more I see
how necessary a residence here is for a young
man, who is utterly unconscious of his own ignorance in a colony, and comforts himself by knowing
as much as his neighbours, which is no very
difficult matter. It will require no common inducement to make me ever return to Ceylon.
Life is not long enough to waste the best part
of it by living away from all the advantages
which civilisation affords, to break up all the ties
one may have formed and which can never be
reunited, to be destitute as well of the means
of improvement as of common information upon
everyday topics."

The record, however, does not long continue in this high tone, and though Laurence always retained a high opinion of the uses of education obtained in the way of social intercourse, he falls lightly into his natural style as his story flows from one dinner-party and festive gathering to another. The progress of the young man, as yet wise enough to listen more than talk, with his lively eyes wide open, and his mind weighing every novelty and taking in every information, is delightful to follow. On one occasion he says : "The conversation, from the beginning of the dinner to the end (there being sixteen or eighteen people), was exclusively confined to speculations upon the future Ministers and Lord Derby's policy ; indeed I have heard so much discussion upon politics in general, and the capacities of various men in particular, that I'll trouble you rather ! and the best thing Lord Derby can do is to recommend the Queen to send for me if she wants advice."

In spring, as in duty bound, Laurence paid his respects to her Majesty, whom he found himself so well qualified to advise. " I have had the honour," he says, " of pressing my lips upon the fingers of royalty. I went through the ordeal with considerable fortitude, following Sir George Pollock. I found nearly everybody was in uniform; the few who were in civil costume looked like servants of the royal household. The Queen looked me in the face much harder than I expected, and I returned the gaze with such a will that I forgot to kneel, ultimately nearly going down on both knees, after which, finding the backing-out process rather irksome, I fairly turned tail and bolted."

It is unnecessary to enter into the politics which he touches so lightly; nor had he as yet any personal connection with them to justify a plunge into that whirlpool of which the older reader will remember the agitations. The period is already too old for contemporary interest, too recent for history. It was the end of a long period of peace; so long, that notwithstanding the convulsions of 1848 upon the Continent, many optimists were still capable of holding the opinion that the reign of war was over, and that under no circumstances could tranquil England bind on her disused armour or draw her rusty sword again. The following note upon the closing of the Great Exhibition of 1851—the first step in the new emulation of arts and crafts and national intercourse, which was to supplant and make warfare impossible, as was fondly supposed—carries us back pleasantly to one of the happier fancies of the time. The great fairy palace, as it was called, in Hyde Park, the temple of glass and iron, which took the public imagination by storm, was still standing, though stripped of its riches, and there was a great movement in favour of retaining it where it had been planted. It is to be supposed that public taste has improved since that time, for the idea of such a construction permanently established in the midst of the trees of Hyde Park is calculated to produce a shuddering horror in most minds nowadays; but that this was by no means the sentiment of the time is very clear. Laurence, indeed, was no authority then or ever from an art point of view; but he expressed a feeling which was very strong in the London of his day when he pronounced energetically for its preservation. Its aspect, he thought, even when despoiled of all its previous attractions, ought to be well noted before any proposal was entertained for its removal. "The miscellaneous crowd—ragged artisans out of work, with Hyde Park dandies, Belgrave Square children playing with those from St Giles', and an orange-woman suckling her child next to a gorgeous matron who looked like a duchess — would be more influential than any number of petitions. It is a mixture of romping, sedateness, and quiet enjoyment."

The mixture of the grave and gay in these delightful letters cannot be better shown than by the extracts that follow, which give at the same time an admirable picture of all the mingled experiences and aspirations of the youth, half-boy, half-man, at the outset of his life. The first is all gaiety, the repetition evidently of a familiar subject of banter between the genial father and son.

Laurence complains, April 23, 1852 :—

"I can't find a single lassie that looks the least as if she would do for a wife, and the article seems so rare that when it presents itself I shall feel bound to snap it up at once for fear of losing it for ever; so beware of hearing unexpectedly of a daughter-in-law. I have been industrious enough to read law until half-past ten at Charles's [Pollock's — now Baron Pollock] chambers one night, but I should apply myself with much more of a will if I was sure of getting business after being called. If I was to go to the Scotch bar, and you were to be made sheriff of some county, we might shake on very comfortably with a farm to amuse you and a railway near."

A little later there follows a pleasant and amusing account of the manner in which he

spends a day, characteristically brought in by
way of showing the worthlessness of the excuse
of business which he has just given as his reason
for not having written to his father. " Tom," it
may be explained, was an old and much beloved
friend, Dr Clark, once surgeon in the 72d High-
landers, and throughout his life devoted to them,
who shared their rooms with Lady Oliphant and
her son.

"My day now is somewhat as follows : I am
up at half-past seven to imbue my mother with
Foster's sound sense, which I do until half-past
eight. At nine we breakfast—viz., Tom and I
—my mother maintaining, in spite of a severe
system of bullying kept up by Tom, her ground,
or rather her room, where she breakfasts. Tom
and I talk politics all breakfast-time, our different
views affording ample matter for discussion, the
idea of a Cobden and Bright Ministry always
driving him frantic. I am then in a proper trim
for the Debates, which I read while digesting,
and then start for chambers, picking up Paul
on the way, and talking about boat - building
and fast men all the way to chambers, when I
begin to read—now on bills of exchange, varying it with abstracting pleadings, for which,
being in the Marshalls' chambers, I am particu-

larly handy. At half-past one I go into Groom's and have 'coffee, brown bread and butter,' in a loud nasal twang. Then say, ' "Punch" after you, sir,' to any man who has got that or any other paper I may want, pay fivepence, and go back to chambers. Walk home with Charles at half-past four discussing law, theology, or politics. Then pay a visit or two, now that the evenings are long, and then most probably home to dress and dine out, and go to a party afterwards, or Royal Institution lectures, or debating society, or opera 'according.' Now, I might write to you instead of reading Foster or the Debates, or paying visits ; so, as I said, want of time is no excuse."

The Foster above referred to is John Foster the essayist, a Nonconformist writer of considerable ability, whose high reputation has suffered some diminution in the course of time.

The political sentiments of a young man brought up as Laurence Oliphant had been were naturally somewhat vague when, fresh from his little colonial world, he suddenly plunged into London ; and his first exposition of his views, as made to his father, are more sentimental than substantial.

"I have become a friend of the people, think

that if they are only trusted they will show themselves worthy of the confidence reposed, that nobody has a right to bully them or pull the Crystal Palace down if they wish it to stay up, and that education and kindness, so far from making Chartists, would make loyal subjects."

This sympathetic feeling developed in his youthful breast in attempts to help and serve those lowest classes in London, who call forth so many enthusiasms and generous efforts, with so little apparent result. His benevolent work began by an expedition made into the slums of Westminster in company with Lady Troubridge and a missionary.

"Not altogether pleasant," he says, "addressing a group of thieves in Old Pye Street. Lady T. seemed to think it quite natural, so I could not well help myself, and insinuated to the least brutal-looking of them that a meeting was going to be held in the next street which they might find interesting, upon which he laughed and asked 'Jim' if he heard that; upon which Jim said that he did, and that he had other meetings to attend rather more to his taste than that, he'd be sworn to, 'not reflectin' noways on you, sir.' Whereupon, after a little chaffing among themselves, they decided it warn't the sort of thing that would suit them, 'no offence to you, ye know, sir'; and one man did me the honour to say that he'd no doubt I meant well. So I went unsuccessfully to the meeting, where I found congregated fifty or sixty fellows who had come in from curiosity, none of whom, to all appearance, had ever been in a church in their lives, and who either stared vacantly or chaffed and made jokes, while here and there a little sparring-match went on."

This first attempt, in which the lively youth found perhaps more amusement than was consistent with the desperate character of the enterprise, would not seem to have been very successful. The service, as he reports it, was conducted with difficulty. A hymn was sung, rather to the amazement of the roughs, and the small congregation was addressed by the missionaries; but as this was done not "very judiciously, they soon got tired."

"Some boys began to fight, and had to be lugged out by their legs and arms, creating a great sensation. Some of the men seemed attentive, however, while others made jokes, and the boys who had been turned out began throwing stones against the windows; so that by the time we got to the next hymn there was a considerable row, which increased as we began it, as everybody began to sing at the top of their voices a variety of airs, amid occasional bursts of laughter. When service was over, some promised to come back, while others went away amused; but all through there was no absolute incivility shown, which, considering the men, was a great deal to say."

He had scarcely thus got himself in train, however, laying out his work, his gaieties, and his attempts at missionary exertion in the way specially favoured at the time, when weariness stole upon him, and dissatisfaction. He discovered that the constant dissipation of a London season is absolutely incompatible with any sufficient amount of legal or any other work. "Gallops in the Park," he says, "when too frequent, rather prevent the proper progress of the law"; and his many other engagements and interests could scarcely fail to bear the same tendency. The length of time required for the training necessary for the English Bar also began to discourage him, and the hope of more ready admittance and better prospects in the North seemed to afford an attractive alternative. He thus announces his changed intention in this respect :—

"LONDON, *June* 7, 1852.

"Thinking it nonsense not looking for myself into the prospects of the Scotch Bar, and as it was impossible to do so satisfactorily without going there, I took a run up in the steamer with Aunt Sophy, who happened to be making the move at the time, and remained just thirty-three hours with Anthony Murray, which I employed looking over the courts and into the faces of the barristers, and thought that they did not express the brieflessness of English lawyers—a suspicion that was confirmed upon my conferring with Robert Oliphant, who said the Scotch Bar never afforded such prospects of advancement as at this moment. Anthony Murray said the same, and the result was that I determined to come to the Scotch Bar as speedily as possible—to effect which a Civil Law examination is required ; and as attendance of classes is not necessary, I am at this moment cramming Justinian with a view to passing on the 3d of next month, as they said that though a year's study was the usual thing, if I chose to stand the trial and could pass it, they did not care for anything else. I have exactly one month to prepare ; but it is worth making the

spurt, as it will be such a saving of time.
Exactly one year hence I shall pass, I hope, in
Scots Law, and be a practising advocate in
Edinburgh long before my terms at this hopeless Bar will be completed. The prizes there
do not seem so far out of one's reach, and I
have every intention of going in for everything
—which I could never screw up my courage to
do here."

He was, however, at the same time fully resolved to keep up his terms at the English Bar
in spite of his Scotch practice, and retain the
valuable connections he had formed there.

In the meantime the little book, chiefly composed of extracts from his diary, about Nepaul,
had been put together and prepared for the
press — though nothing is said about it in the
letters until its appearance is recorded. The book
was ready in the early spring of 1852, and confided to "Uncle Tom" for revision. This was Mr
Thomas Oliphant, the youngest brother of Sir
Anthony, well known in connection with music,
and the author of some popular songs. There is
no information as to this gentleman's literary
gifts; but in those days no one was aware, himself least of all, that young Laurence was to be
one of the most popular writers of his time,

and his anxious mother thought it a great matter that the boy's book should be looked over and licked into shape by a more experienced hand. "I have handed over your manuscript to Mr Murray," says the uncle, "after having carefully gone through it and made such alterations as will in many cases cause it to read better. The mere unpremeditated language of a diary won't do for appearing in print. It gives a flippant character to the style of the narrative, and is apt to weary the reader. With such further alterations as I have no doubt Mr Murray's reader will think it necessary to make, the book will be very interesting, and likely to do you credit." "I send you the above," writes Lady Oliphant to her husband in great satisfaction, "hoping it will please you to see your brother's opinion of Lowry's book." Whether Lowry himself was equally pleased with the prospect of being subjected to the alterations of "Mr Murray's reader" does not appear; but he shows no such vanity about his first appearance in print as is general with young authors—regarding it, so far as can be seen, from a most business-like and practical point of view. He sent out to his father, apparently for the use of Ceylon, fifty copies, and his report of his first venture is made in the most moderate terms, and without any of the usual excitement of young authorship.

"I shall send my book by the Queen of the South," he says. "Two thousand copies have already (ten days) been sold out of the three thousand which formed the first edition, and I have had long and favourable notices in the 'Athenæum,' 'Economist,' 'Examiner,' and 'Literary Gazette,' in which papers look (date about last week in May). It seems to give very general satisfaction, and I hope to have another edition out in a month or two."

This is all that the young writer says about his first performance. It was published in a cheap form, and brought him, I believe, very little profit, though some praise.

In the middle of the summer of 1852 he had taken up his quarters in Edinburgh, and was in full progress of study and equally high spirits, "cramming" for the examination, which was to take place on the 3d of the ensuing month, with great hopes of success. His preliminary steps are amusing.

"I have been introduced to all my examiners, and have buttered them properly, and they look good-natured enough. Robert Oliphant has been overwhelming me with kindness — introducing me right and left, propitiating my examiners,

and puffing me splendidly as a colonial lawyer,
a young author, and altogether an interesting
young personage, that it would be folly to pluck
for the want of a little smattering of Latin."

His future companions are described with similar light-hearted satisfaction.

"The more I see of this Bar, the more I prefer
it to England — it is so much more snug and
sociable; and though there is a considerable
sprinkling of snobs, yet there are some gentlemen, and they shine out all the more conspicu-
ously, and indeed get more business on that
account. It is evidently the correct thing to
be a high Tory here, so remember I won't pledge
myself to any opinions."

The next event in his life was the success of his
Civil Law examination.

"The examiners were evidently in a much
greater fright of puzzling themselves than anything else, and in the Civil Law they skimmed
the surface in very safe questions : decidedly
the most trying part was the walking in before
seven great fellows sitting round a table in
solemn wigs. However, they shook hands with
me with great cordiality, welcoming me among
them and passing me unanimously, which was
nothing more than they ought to have done, seeing I never made a mistake. The whole thing

did not last half an hour, and I sent a message down to my mother by electric telegraph, which reached her in half an hour more."

The opinion he had formed of Edinburgh society in those days does not seem to have been a high one, but yet he managed to console himself in many ways.

"I think Edinburgh is such a beautiful town that I am fully compensated for its dulness by its romance, and shall have so many friends near that I can always run over to Keir, Blair Drummond, Abercairney, or Ochtertyre—from all which places I have received invitations—to say nothing of Condie, and Freeland, only two hours from Edinburgh. I think it rather an advantage that Edinburgh offers no attraction in the way of society. Notwithstanding this, I find myself dining out every night, the last place being with old Colonel Phillpott and family. Curiously enough, I met at the station, all in the same carriage, Algernon Egerton, Campbell of Monzie, Sir Alexander Mackenzie, and Hawkins, an Indian judge, all of whom I had known, and none of whom hardly knew one another. . . . Campbell of Monzie, worn out with his week's canvassing, was going for the Sunday to Monzie, and took advantage of his audience to explain his principles,

which he did as if he were a Free Kirk minister,
thumping the side of the carriage cushion when
he grew vehement in his advocacy of Protestant
doctrines, and by his explanations of the 'truth
as it is in Jesus' seeking to impress upon us the
principles as they were in Monzie. He has a
smart, amusing way of answering, and told us a
story of having canvassed a man who seemed
adverse to give him his vote, and was in fact
rather grumpy and gruff in his refusal to do so,
whereupon Campbell said, 'But if you don't vote
for me, who will you vote for?' whereupon the
man said he would sooner vote for the devil; on
which Campbell answered, 'Well, if your friend
should not come forward, perhaps you will give
me your vote.'"

In another letter he describes his experiences
in the office of his relation Mr Robert Oliphant,
a Writer to the Signet in Edinburgh, and gives
an account of his day's work, which has a great
air of diligence :—

"Everybody overwhelms me with kindness,
and I am in great luck to be taken into Robert
Oliphant's office on the free-and-easy terms I am ;
for I am not set down to copy useless papers, but
simply to learn the routine. The clerks take a

great interest in me, and explain the forms, &c.
I go to the Parliament House at nine with the
P. H. clerk, and see what is going on, listen to
cases I have previously read in the office, and
talk to the various counsel, most of whom I know
now. Moreover, it is useful to be known and
seen often about those purlieus. After an hour
or two there I come down to the office, where I
remain till four, when I go and attend the Con-
veyancing class of Professor Menzies. I don't
think lectures do one much good. I can get up
more in a given time by reading ; so I have given
up the Scots Law. . . . There are really no
clever men at the Bar now coming on, but the
juniors are a remarkably nice set of fellows. The
Lord Advocate, Inglis, is a very sharp chap and a
good speaker, and out and out the cleverest man
at the bar. So that there is a great opening, and
Robert Oliphant promises he will give me business
as soon as I am called, so that it will be my own
fault if I do not get on. Everything seems much
simpler than in England, and business is carried
on in a nice familiar style, of which the following
dialogue is a sort of sample :—

"*Mr Mackenzie, loq.*—There is a case just
precisely similar to this one, my lord, I might
say upon a' fours with it, which ye'll find in
Dunlop, but I'll no' trouble ye with it i' the

noo. . . . Your lordship 'll maybe no' sit to-morrow ?

"*Lord Robertson.*—And why not, Mr Mackenzie ? I think I'm as well sittin' here as anywhere else ?

"*Mr Mac.*—I was thinking, it being a particular occasion, out of respect for his Grace's interment——

"*Lord Rob.*—I'm no' wanting in respec' for the Duke ; but I'd sooner be here than at the funeral, and I'll just sit as usual."

Many readers will remember the jovial and jocular judge, the

> "Lord Peter,
> Who feared not God nor man nor metre,"

who is the hero of this story,—one of the last Lords of Session by whom " braid Scots" was still occasionally spoken.

Laurence and his mother, who had accompanied him, occupied during their residence in Edinburgh at this time rooms in North Castle Street, a locality rendered classical by the long dwelling in it of Sir Walter Scott. Sir Anthony Oliphant had all a Scotsman's admiration and half-sentimental longing for Edinburgh as a residence, and his son's exhortation, " Do come home," had doubtless all the more force as coming from that romantic and beloved city. "We should all be much more comfortable," the young man adds; "and," recurring to the old joke, "I could begin to look out for a wife under your auspices. I don't see any likelihood of finding one for myself."

Shortly after, however, we find him again in London, whither he went periodically to "eat his terms," and where he recurs to the "black-guards," his *protégés* in Westminster. The movement on behalf of reformed or reformable thieves was then in an *accès* of energy, taken up vigorously under the patronage of Lord Shaftesbury, with much accompaniment of midnight meetings, and a considerable amount of excitement. Among other incitements to a life of industry, a number of these men had been set to cutting wood for firewood, and Laurence was much concerned to prove that in patronising this effort the public in general was not incurring the reproach of taking bread out of honest people's mouths.

"If we make a man who has hitherto been dishonest, honest, instead of being a burden to the State, he is a supporter of it, and a cheaper article in that capacity in the long-run, though it may cost something to make him honest. That strange obliquity of moral vision which makes a large portion of the community Tories, prevents them from apprehending this. The problem is evidently 'How is a reformatory not a premium on vice?' We are now experimentally solving it. It seems to me that there should be some place where, when a man is bankrupt in character, he might go and get whitewashed—some probation through which when he passes he should come out registered A 1 in point of respectability. At present if a man sinks below a certain level in this country, unless some one takes him by the hand, no individual efforts on his part will raise him above it."

One of the meetings which followed the industrial experiment is described as follows: "The whole thing was very striking; and I felt, while a whole room full of the worst characters in London were singing 'God save the Queen' or 'I will arise,' that I ought to have wept, and that you certainly would have. It is so difficult to realise the depravity of the men who are so innocently employed, and in whose countenances you can detect the hard lines which a vicious life has imprinted, but which are rapidly becoming softened by their voluntary subjection to a life of restraint and honest industry. It is the most interesting thing I have ever seen."

In the August of 1852 Laurence made use of

his first vacation in a Continental tour most happily and fortunately directed, at first designed as a mere expedition in pursuit of sport, but turning afterwards to much more important issues. His companion was Mr Oswald Smith, one of the great banking family of Smith, Payne, & Smith, between whom and the Oliphants there was an old family connection, which had introduced Laurence to the house of a member of the firm, on his first arrival in England. The youth who thus accompanied him in one of his earliest adventures, contributed, nearly half a century after, a brief but interesting memoir of his lifelong friend to one of the Magazines on Laurence's death—and naturally this boyish expedition occupies a large place in it. Mr Smith is perhaps unduly contemptuous of the gifts as a sportsman of one who had ranged the jungles of Ceylon in his boyhood, and hunted elephants with Jung Bahadour; but that the young man, already familiar with such exploits, should look for a fresh and unhackneyed field, something less tame than a moor in Scotland or the banks of a Norwegian fiord, was natural enough; and he was also in search of "something to write about"—a very legitimate object, if seldom so honestly avowed. "The only part of Europe within reach fulfilling the required condition," Laurence himself says in the 'Episodes,' "seemed

to me the Russian Lapland : for I heard from an
Archangel merchant that the Kem and other
rivers in that region swarmed with guileless
salmon who had never been offered a fly, and
that it would be easy to cross to Spitzbergen to
get a shot at some white bears."

As it turned out, this chance project proved of
the very highest importance in the young adventurer's life, and set him well afloat upon the career
of public service, tempered with personal fancy, in
which so many years were to be passed. When
the two young men reached St Petersburg they
were allowed to go no farther in their equipment
as sportsmen—though whether by actual prohibi-
tion, or because of the excessive duty demanded
on their fishing-gear and equipments, is not quite
clear. Mr Smith adds that they were too late
in the year to go north with any chance of sport.
"It may give some idea," he says, " of Oliphant's
sanguine and imaginative character, to record
that his plan for future proceedings was to dis-
embark on the right bank of the Volga at Tsait-
sin, not far from Astracan, and ride over the Don
Cossack steppe, four hundred miles, to Taganrog,
on the Azof Sea." They did do something like
this, driving in rude native carriages, and finally
reached the Crimea, then an unknown and un-
explored peninsula, and the mysterious city of

Sebastopol, of which many legends, but no definite and clear information, had reached the world. It was known that Russia was there establishing an arsenal and headquarters of war, from which she would be able to descend upon Turkey and overawe Europe; that the entry was forbidden to strangers, and any attempt to make acquaintance with the place dangerous; —all excellent reasons why the young travellers should push their way thither, which they did after all without much difficulty. Thus the "something to write about" was most successfully attained.

We find a full account of this journey in the letters to Lady Oliphant, beginning with the very first steps from home. At Berlin they paused for a day or two, and Laurence takes the opportunity to express his satisfaction with his travelling companion, in a charming and playful note full of boyish appreciation and fun. "It is a great thing having with one so handsome a young Engländer, as all the pretty girls look our way, and I am humble enough to be quite content with the side-glances I thus get, he being quite unconscious of his own attractions." It may be added that Laurence was by no means unqualified " to please a damsel's eye " in his own person, and was almost certain to be, under any circumstances, the most entertaining

and attractive person in his neighbourhood wherever he was.

"The first thing that astonishes you as you
land are the droskies and their drivers. The former
are only capable generally of holding one person
besides the driver, behind whom the passenger
sits cross-legged, somewhat in that way [a sketch
is here given], if you can understand this illustration. The latter are rigged up in caps like
this [with another sketch], and long dressing-
gowns, and longer red beards, and always give
you the benefit of their flavour as you sit behind
them. The chief difficulty, however, consists in
maintaining your seat over the pavement, which
is execrable. In fact, the only things that are
old in the town are the droskies and the pavement—everything else wears an unpleasantly new
and fresh appearance; and the builders of the
city have fallen into the mistake, though it is one
on the right side, of leaving the spaces in front
of the public buildings immensely large, so that
the stray man or drosky which you see wandering about them gives one the impression of the
city only being half full. Still I have never seen
anything to equal the *coup d'œil* from the bridge,
facing the Izak Church and the Winter Palace,
certainly the finest of royal residences in Europe.

The Neva is as broad as the Thames, and beautifully clear, and the quays are handsome and substantial: however, Murray's handbook describes the town much better than I can, and unless we have some adventures up country, I shall have nothing to write about."

In spite of this fear, he manages as usual to give a very picturesque account of their evening visit to the Mineral Waters, whither they went in a steamer :—

"Shooting through bridges, the arches of which were so small that you could easily touch the key-stone as you stood on deck, or, leaning over either side, touch the stone buttresses: it required the most beautiful steering; I don't think there was six inches to spare in any direction. Our boat-load consisted of a crowd going up to the Mineral Waters, a place of evening resort during the summer months, and which was as beautifully got up as Vauxhall. However, it was too like it to be interesting: the display of fireworks at the end was grand enough. We went to see a ceremony in the Greek Church the other night, and the prostrations beat those of the most devout and enthusiastic of Mussulmans. It was a very picturesque sight to see the men tossing their long hair and beards about as they flung their heads up and down."

The next day, after driving to a place called Gorilla, where they slept, they "mounted horses which had been sent out there for us, and rode eight miles to Krasnoe-Selo plain, where the Emperor was to manœuvre 80,000 men, a grand sham fight with the whole Russian army, to close the summer inspections."

"The whole way to the plains the white tents of the camp extended, and when we reached a rising ground we had a magnificent view. On a knoll near us was the Emperor with a brilliant staff, which any Englishman in uniform might join unasked : unfortunately we were obliged to keep a respectful distance, but saw none the worse on that account. 40,000 men under Sidigri advanced, and after some hard cannonading with 40,000 under the Emperor, and a great deal of dashing about of cavalry and horse-artillery, drove the opposite hosts behind some further trenches. Altogether I never had so good an idea of a battle before. Sometimes the whole mass was moving at once, and the position in which we were enabled us to see everything perfectly. The most beautiful corps were the Circassian horse, covered with armour, and the Cossacks, with their long beards and spears dashing in all directions. We were nearly carried away by a charge of hussars, and only escaped by sheltering ourselves behind a friendly house."

On the following day Laurence announced the definite change of their plans, about which they had been uncertain; but "the custom-house has most kindly helped us out of our dilemma by deliberately and coolly charging us £15 duty on our rods and guns, which our prudence at once prevented our thinking of paying." This, however, he thinks he can avoid, according to the advice of the Financial Minister, by taking them to Finland, a country which he has determined to visit, and which is not yet under the Russian custom laws. "So that we are not altogether sold; but meantime, as there is no such hurry now that we have given up the shores of the White Sea, we are first going to take a run down to the grand fair of Nijni Novgorod, and spending a couple of days *en retour* at Moscow." He regards this extra expenditure as justifiable, as he looks upon his journey as "a distinct system of self-education."

"Though I must own that I have not been

able to find out much that is really interesting in a country and government which I
have always looked upon as likely to afford
more information than any other in Europe,
further than the palpable hindrance which the
policy of the Government offers to anything
like advancement or civilisation where it is most
needed. I don't think we have anything to fear
from Russia : its gigantic proportions render it
so unwieldy, and the people are so barbarous,
that we shall always have the same advantages which our enlightenment gives us over
the Eastern nations. I look upon it as little
better than China : the only difference is that
usually barbarous nations hold civilised nations
in respect, which, to judge from the way they
bully you in the custom-house, Russia does not."

The next letter is dated from Moscow, "this
most charming of cities."

" If ever there was a town that would bear to
be written about it is this, decidedly ranking with
Khatmandhu or Cairo in general novelty, while it
is far before either in its particular objects of
interest. . . . The Kremlin itself is the most
unique and picturesque assemblage of churches
and palaces of ancient and modern art, and of

Eastern and Western architecture, that could be
found anywhere collected in so small a compass,
and so happily grouped together. The gilded
domes and cupolas might be in the Punjaub,
while the palace which they adjoin might be in
Paris. The church of St Basil is perfectly unlike
anything old or new, occidental or oriental, and
forms a most striking foreground to one of the
views of the Kremlin, which I hope some day to
show you."

After this a forty-eight hours' diligence journey
brought the two friends to Nijni Novgorod, where
the great fair was going on.

" Your letter reached me in the shop of Aaron,
a Jew from Bukharia, who was regaling us with
almonds, dried peas, and raisins in his warehouse
in the great fair, and displaying the wonders that
come from that part of the world. Indeed it would
be difficult to think of a part of the world that did
not contribute something to this Russian emporium, and I have no doubt that before I have
done exploring I shall find a coir-mat and
perhaps a Moorman to sell it me. . . . I was
rather disappointed in seeing no Chinese, and, in
fact, not quite as great a variety of costume as I
expected ; but the variety of goods disposed for

sale compensates in a great measure for this, and though not so striking at first, is as satisfactory when one comes to examine the shops and overhaul their contents."

By some mistake of the steamboat company's agent, Laurence and Smith were detained at Nijni Novgorod two days later than they expected, and consequently outstayed the first freshness of interest. In his next letter he complains—

" It is a great bore, when one wants to do as much as possible in a given time, to be kept in a place after you have seen as much as you want of it. Nor can I make as good use of my time as I might. I am very much left to myself to pick up my information as I best can, and that is only by my eyes, since the merchants are too busy to attend to one, and too stupid to give any valuable information upon matters that from their vocation they ought to know something of. To-day, therefore, having seen every part of the fair, we took to drawing, and found some lovely views. The old town overhangs the Volga most picturesquely, and from the cliffs an extensive view is obtained in all directions, and a very interesting one over the flat on which the fair is situated, quite unlike anything I ever saw before. The view was too difficult and complicated for me to attempt: the two rivers Oka and Volga looked alive with human beings, as well as the peninsula on which 150,000 people are hived like bees. . . . I would not have missed this fair on any account, though I would not advise everybody to make the journey from Moscow *exprès* — whereas I should almost say my father would consider it worth a journey from England alone."

He goes on : " I must tell you what we propose doing, instead of hovering in a desultory way about the fair, having already occupied half the day in writing a description of it, which differs so much from that given in Murray's handbook that I don't think he will approve it at all. First, then, there being two companies of steamers lately started on the river for the purpose of towing barges up and down it, and not of carrying passengers we are going to take advantage of them, but must submit to the inconvenience of going slowly, and of starting on no fixed day, but when the barges are ready. Still, as the accommodation is most comfortable, and as nobody that I know except the inhabitants of this part of the world has been down the Volga, we are going to try it, hoping that it may pay in the way of interest. The river being low, we shall not go very fast, and shall probably not get to Zaritzen, our point of debarkation, under ten or twelve days, during which time we must amuse ourselves as best we can. I regret that I did not buy some solid books at Moscow, but I did not then anticipate wanting one. You will see in the map that where the Volga takes its last bend towards the Caspian, the Don approaches within fifty or sixty miles of it, and trends away to the Sea of Azof. Here we cross, and embarking in a boat, glide down this river, if we find it practicable and convenient (there being no steamer) to Taganrog. At any rate, there is a post-road if we prefer it. Then a steamer will take us on to Kertch, from which place we ride through the Crimea to Sevastopol, and then *viâ* Odessa to Vienna and home. . . . The Crimea, at any rate, I know to be well worth seeing. We should have liked Astrakhan and the Caspian, and across *viâ* Tiflis, but have no time; and Astrakhan is a mere Russian town, not half so well worth seeing as one would imagine from its name."

The next letter is written on the Volga, which, in his usual enthusiastic way, he describes as

" this most magnificent of rivers." The account of their life on board the steamer is given at length : they were the only passengers.

" We have exclusive possession of the after-part of a ship, having a sumptuous cabin, a nice dining-room on deck, and a good storeroom for our necessaries. It was rather an interesting matter providing for the start ; for not having a servant, we were obliged to make our purchases ourselves, and rushed about buying bread and meat and groceries, ultimately attaining a considerable proficiency in making bargains. We fortunately have the use of the captain's cook, but do every-thing else ourselves, and are expert in laying the table, giving out the necessary stores, and econo-mising our small means. Hardly anything is to be procured at the villages on the banks. This morning we made a tour of inspection of our larder, and found thirty out of fifty hard-boiled eggs had been broken and were bad, and the ham had been put in a damp place and got mouldy : however, we hope to make something of it ; but the eggs, alas ! are gone for ever. The experience which we have gained in sundry do-mestic matters, however, will be useful to us hereafter, if we marry unfortunately — as my father did."

This latter little piece of *espiègleric*, as well as the continued and delightful references to his father, are very characteristic of the terms on which the young man stood with both his adoring parents.

After complaining that the speed of the voyage down the Volga was not quite regular, as the barges sometimes drew more water than the steamers and ran aground, when " we lug away for a considerable time to get them off," he goes on :—

" The river is so low that we shall take longer to get to Zaritzen than 1 anticipated, and I may as well warn you in time not to expect me home before the 20th October. I shall be anxious to hear at Odessa what news from Ceylon. Our voyage down the Don I look forward to with great pleasure. The whole tour will be a novel one, and I hope it may furnish sufficient incidents and matter to be interesting in some shape or other to the public.

" We are at this moment hard and fast on a *pericarte* or sandbank, and there is no telling how long we may remain where we are. Yesterday we stuck on one for nine hours. When we pass this one, and another one or two, our difficulties will be over, and we shall get rapidly on.

We are towing two immense barges, each 320 feet long, and the current is eternally setting them on the shallows, much to our disgust. However, this is not called a passenger steamer, and we were prepared for these delays, so we cannot grumble : besides, except for the temporary annoyance caused by them, we could not be more delightfully comfortable. Our existence approaches to perfection to my mind — gliding quietly along under high wooded banks, past romantic glens and picturesque villages, along the noblest river in Europe ; the days beautiful, the climate bracing, the thermometer ranging between 52° in the morning and 72° in the middle of the day ; with a walk and a sketch of an afternoon when we stop to take in wood. We have all the elements of a comfortable existence except clean linen. Our larder certainly is not very extensive, and we are most abstemious in the matter of drink, taking nothing but tea and Volga. Still, there is a considerable pleasure in laying one's own table-cloth, and bringing out one's stores, and eating them in contentment.

"I do not remember ever having read an account of this part of the world, or of the country of the Don Cossacks, through which we are going. Many of the villages here are composed purely of Tartars, and they are as unlike Russians as Eng-

lish—in fact, they remind me more of the Bootyas
in Nepaul than any other people. Their dress is
very curious, and the women wear gold coins in
their hair and silver breastplates. The men
look just like what Chinese gipsies would be, if
such animals existed, swarthy instead of copper-
coloured, with Chinese features."

Sometimes they see "a train of seven or eight
barges wind slowly up the river tugged by a
huge leading barge containing 150 horses and as
many men, the latter employed in laying out
anchors ahead, the former in going round a cap-
stan as they would in a threshing-machine, and
warping the barges up to the anchors."

" You will be glad to hear," he adds, " that we
have at last overcome or undergone all *pericartes*,
and that we are getting merrily along, with bright
sunshiny days. This afternoon we hope to arrive
at Simbirsk, a town which ought to be marked
on the map as the capital of a province. I enjoyed my ramble over the old Tartar capital very
much, and had a very magnificent view from the
Kremlin walls. I hope the waiter to whom I
confided my letter posted it, as it contained much
information which I cannot now repeat. . . . I
shall not write again after leaving Simbirsk until

I get to Taganrog. I have got so much to draw and so much journal to write and so little to tell, that I shall do no more now than repeat that I could not be happier or enjoying myself more."

This last threat is not exactly carried out, as we find Laurence writing again from Saratov. He complains, though not angrily, of the frequent delays when detained "by people who do not understand expedition or regularity, and at whose mercy we must be so completely." These vexations were, however, balanced by the amiability of his companion, who never complained, though he had a perfect right to do so, seeing that he came out for a sporting expedition, and had been carried off instead to explore unknown wilds, much more satisfactory to Laurence, whose desire to find "something to write about" was never absent from his mind.

At last, on the 20th of September, the friends arrived at Taganrog, having finished the still more exciting land journey.

"It is with feelings of unmitigated satisfaction that I date my letter from here, after having accomplished in five days and nights one of the most wild, uncouth, and unfrequented journeys that even Russia can boast.

I confess that the prospect of a steppe journey through the country of the Don Cossacks
was a little appalling to us, not knowing a
word of the language, or able to find a single
person who had ever been on the road or could
give us any information upon it. Our scheme
for going down the Don was quite impracticable with our limited time, and so we decided
to buy a carriage at Dubofskoi, where we left
the steamer, and get across somehow from the
banks of the Volga to the shores of the Sea of
Azof: there was no alternative between doing
this and going on to Astrakhan and then across
the Caucasus by Tiflis, which would have taken
an indefinite time. Fortunately, even at such an
out-of-the-way place as Dubofskoi, we found a
carriage, for which we had to pay about £11,
and launched ourselves upon the steppe. It was
a sort of post-road, and every fifteen or twenty
miles was a wooden hut, with a sort of kraal for
horses behind. The country was like the sea,
with a heavy ground-swell on and calm surface,
being covered with a short dry grass. Often for
miles not a creature was seen ; sometimes bullock-
carts passed us, or a wild Cossack galloped by on
horseback, and here and there latterly villages
came pretty thick, with round houses like the
haystacks with which they were always sur-

rounded, and from which you could hardly distinguish them, or ragged - looking cabins like those in an Irish village, from which issued wild independent - looking unshaven creatures. The road was often a mere track across the grass, and the country presented the exact same appearance for so long a time as to become quite wearisome. On arriving at a station, we generally saw no one but a woman or a child or two, one of whom went and called a man, who immediately mounted on one of our last team and galloped across the steppe, bringing back in half an hour or so six or eight horses, which he drove into the kraal at full gallop, selected three, took half an hour or more to harness them, and then went off with us at a full gallop. Luckily the road was generally smooth, but we occasionally dashed down ugly places, the result of which was that at last one of the wheels was so near coming off that we had to stay a night at a post-station—a rest we were not sorry to take, though it was on a wooden stretcher; but a sheepskin I bought has on sundry occasions made a capital mattress, only it retains the fleas for a long time. Our great stand-by was the *samovar*, or hot-water urn for making tea, with which the poorest peasant is always supplied. Except a little meat at starting, we lived entirely on hard-boiled eggs, rusks, and cheese, comforting ourselves with some capital tea which we bought at Nijni. Not a thing besides hot water was to be procured the whole way, but the people were very civil, though rough and barbarous : they seemed honest, but I saw so few of them I could not judge much about them one way or another. . . . Altogether, though the country was as uninteresting as an Egyptian desert, and we were dead beat and as universally shaken and nearly coming to pieces as our carriage, yet there is some satisfaction in having successfully made so outlandish a journey alone. . . . Luckily our carriage stood it wonderfully, another wheel just coming off as we entered the inn-yard."

At Taganrog the two young men heard to their dismay that instead of two steamers a-week to Kertch there was but one a fortnight, an arrangement which seemed to make the journey so painfully and courageously performed a failure as to its final object. It is almost sulkily, though with the native humour, somewhat angry this time, peeping through, that Laurence complains : " Everything is badly arranged in this country ; nobody knows anything, and every piece of information relative to travelling has been invariably quite wrong. I had hoped to see the Crimea quite comfortably, and now doubt whether we shall have time to do it at all ; but everybody says it is the thing most well worth seeing in Russia, which will rather reconcile me to missing it, as most probably this is a lie too."

I am sorry to say that here the letters end : and the reader must be referred for the further course of the journey and the inspection of Sebastopol which followed — by no means of such engrossing interest now as it was then—to the narrative published in the following year. The purpose of finding something to write about was most triumphantly fulfilled, if not the sporting expedition, which was to one of the travellers, at least, so much less important. We can only hope that Mr Smith too was consoled for the big game he did not shoot, and the salmon he did not catch, by the humours and wonders of this wild extraordinary journey.

CHAPTER IV.

AMERICA AND CANADA.

It is needless to explain how extremely important this boyish expedition—lightly undertaken indeed, yet not without that shrewd and clear-sighted apprehension of coming events which, with all the gaiety and all the daring love of adventure, love of fun, eager pursuit under all and through all of new experiences, both in life and thought, was an inherent part of Oliphant's many-sided nature—was in the story of his life. The Crimea was a country unknown, and Sebastopol a wonder and mystery even while all the elements were working together to precipitate our troops upon its shores. " In the middle of this century," says Mr Kinglake,[1] in the beautiful description of the

---

[1] These lines were written while that accomplished historian and traveller was still with us, and when the hope of his ever-kind and ready interest was present with the writer, as his friendship and sympathy had always been with the subject of this memoir. There have been many voices to recall the wonderful force of that unique

Chersonese peninsula with which his history opens, " the peninsula which divides the Euxine from the Sea of Azoff was an almost forgotten land, lying out of the chief paths of merchants and travellers, and far away from all the capital cities of Christendom. Rarely went thither any one from Paris, or Vienna, or Berlin : to reach it from London was a harder task than to cross the Atlantic ; and a man of office receiving in this distant province his orders despatched from St Petersburg, was the servant of masters who governed him from a distance of a thousand miles."

This was the distance which the young explorers had traversed ; and in the course of the next year their experiences were laid before the public in the book called the ' Russian Shores of the Black Sea,' which was really almost the only work in which the British reader could ascertain what was the country, and what the special difficulties of the war upon the verge of which Great Britain was now trembling. That it was received with extreme interest, and at once secured the general attention, is clear from the fact that on the 4th of March 1854 a fourth edition was called for and

and elaborate study of modern warfare which filled his later life, and the airy and sparkling record of picturesque travel which conferred a blaze of fame upon his youth. The gentleness of his age, the tenderness of his sympathy, his ever-indulgent criticism and delightful praise, are recollections still more intimate and dear.

in the press. By this time the fact that such a book existed, and that two young men in London had penetrated into these unknown but so important regions, seems to have slowly arrived at the consciousness of the authorities, and on a memorable day Laurence was raised into sudden excitement and a fever of hopes and expectations by a summons to the Horse Guards, to meet the generals who were anxiously employed in the construction of plans for the campaign, in order to give them all the information he could on the subject. He talks in one letter of "Oswald rushing in waving a letter over his head," and on another occasion of "a mounted orderly" who rattled up to his door, dazzling all the lodging-houses in Half-Moon Street, with a mission from these great men. The summons was to the effect that "Lord Raglan wanted to see me at once." He communicates this briefly to his father as follows :—

"I accordingly proceeded to the Ordnance, where I found not Lord Raglan, but Lord de Ros, who questioned me minutely about Sebastopol. I gave him all the information I could, and sent him my sketches, extracts from my journal, and everything I could think useful. There were a couple of old Engineer Colonels (one of them afterwards identified as Sir John Burgoyne), all three poring over a chart of the Crimea. They are evidently going to try and take Sebastopol, and I recommended their landing at Balaclava and marching across, which I think they will do. Lord de Ros was immensely civil. I think Lord Raglan ought in civility to make me his civil secretary. It would be great fun. I met Lord de Ros again this morning, and had a long talk with him. I did not mention my anxiety to get out. It is very ticklish saying anything about one's self on such occasions, and I must just bide my time and qualify myself —be able to answer the lash, as you always say."

The excitement and eager hope produced by these interviews may be imagined. It was almost impossible for the young man to believe that nothing would come of them. He plunged into the study of Turkish, and read everything he could lay his hands on to qualify himself for whatever share might come to him in the tremendous enterprise, for which the country, so long unused to war, and with her sword more or less rusty in its scabbard, was with great general excitement preparing. Laurence had been, almost from the moment of his arrival in England, and notwithstanding his law studies and preliminary work in that profession, avowedly seeking his fortune, with a keen eye upon the horizon for anything that might turn up. He had already leaped into a considerable literary connection. Mr John Blackwood, the editor of the well-known Magazine, a man of remarkable literary perception and insight, had at once divined an invaluable contributor in the young writer; and he had also formed a connection with the 'Daily News,' then a new paper, sparkling with literary life and interest, the first competitor of the 'Times.' His first arrangement with this newspaper was that he should contribute articles at two guineas a column; but when he felt the wave under him floating him upwards, Laurence, who had always a most clear and practical business faculty, thought this remuneration to be inadequate, and in the same letter which describes his interview with the generals he informs his father that he had "called at the 'Daily News' office and said I could not afford to write at two guineas a column, so they offered to double it on the spot: terms which I accordingly accepted, and have knocked off twelve guineas' worth last week. I cannot always carry on at this rate, however, as I run dry. As it is, I am obliged to write bosh occasionally, which I don't like doing; but the public are so gullible, that it is difficult to resist the temptation."

The new hope, however, carried him away from all his existing interests. " I hear nothing but the Eastern question talked of now," he says; " and as I am appealed to as an authority, although I originally knew nothing more about it than my neighbours, I have got it up carefully, in order to answer expectations." He was, however, by no means idle in respect to charitable and philanthropic engagements even during this time of suspense. " On Monday I have to deliver a lecture to what is anticipated to be a crowded audience upon reformatory institutions; on Tuesday to make a speech at a public meeting for the Belgravian Ragged Schools; on Wednesday to a large soiree to meet the swells who take an interest in these things. Last Sunday I gave an address to my blackguards at Westminster." Thus his hands were full as he stood and waited for fate.

The immediate decision came, as often happens, in an entirely unexpected way. He had long entertained hopes of the help and patronage of Lord Elgin, with whose family, and especially with his sisters Lady Charlotte Locker and Lady Augusta Bruce (afterwards Stanley), Lady Oliphant had warm relations of friendship; and it was in the midst of the excitements of the Crimean question, when his attention was wholly bent in another direction, that these hopes suddenly came to fruit. He was hanging amid alternate hopes and fears, " extremely anxious to take part in the Crimean campaign in some capacity or other," and ready to " accept an offer of the late Mr Delane to go out as 'Times' correspondent, had not Lord Clarendon kindly held out hopes that he would send me when an opportunity offered," when promotion came in this totally different quarter. " It was while anxiously awaiting this that Lord Elgin proposed that I should accompany him to Washington on special diplomatic service as secretary ; and as the mission seemed likely to be of short duration I gladly accepted the offer, in the hope that I might be back in time to find employment in the East before the war was over." His expectation was realised, as will be seen, notwithstanding that the length of his absence exceeded his calculations, and his position latterly was more important than he had expected. Thus after fixing all his thoughts upon the East, he was carried off in an exactly opposite direction, and began his active work with all the interest and excitement of a rapid and special mission, in the New World, with which in after-life he was to have so much and so close connection.

During this period of absence the letters of
Lady Oliphant, addressed to her son in America,
afford a companion picture to his minute and
careful record. The mother's anxious prayers
for her only child, her fears for him, her expressions of confidence, her intense longing for his
spiritual improvement and growth in grace, reveal as in a mirror the tender woman's pious and
sensitive soul, and her absorption in her son's
interests and fortunes. Still more interesting
and individual, perhaps (for religious longings
and counsels are inevitably much alike, to whom-
soever addressed), is the cheerful background of
the temporary home in Edinburgh, where her
husband by this time had joined her, and in
which the humour and good spirits of Sir Anthony brightened the whole scene, though he too
could think of nothing so much as his absent son.
Before he left Ceylon on his final retirement
from office, the father had communicated to his
wife and son his readiness to follow the fortunes
of the beloved boy. " I do not know," he says,
" that I have ever clearly expressed myself, but
if not, fully understand that I am quite prepared
to go to any place in Europe to which Lowry
may go, whether as *attaché* or anything else. So
long as it pleases God to spare us, let us all stick
together." The parents remained in Edinburgh

till Lowry should return from his American mission, waiting to see what Providence might have in store for him, and fully determined to carry out this purpose. One can scarcely help the question, whether the lively and adventurous young man would have been made much happier by their determination, or if the thought of his father and mother following him everywhere in his erratic course might not have appeared a little embarrassing as well as ludicrous. The old Judge, however, repeated his intention to some of his friends in Edinburgh in a more humorous way. " The wife is buttoned to Lowry's coat-tails," he said, " and I am tied to her apron-strings. I am just like the last carriage in a train, waggling after them just where they please to lead." They looked forward to some permanent appointment for Lowry, in London perhaps best, with their own house open to all who could serve or please him, and the beloved son coming and going. For Sir Anthony at least this dream of happiness was never to come true.

A full account of Laurence's first experiences in diplomacy has been written by himself in his ' Episodes in a Life of Adventure,' and it is a very amusing chapter. The object of the mission was to negotiate a commercial treaty between Canada and the United States, and in the execution of a piece of business so serious, and which was supposed so unlikely to succeed, Lord Elgin and his staff approached the representatives of the American nation with all the legitimate wiles of accomplished and astute diplomacy. They threw themselves into the society of Washington—which in those days was apparently much more racy and original than it seems to be now, when American statesmen have grown dull, correct, and dignified like other men — with the *abandon* and enjoyment of a group of visitors solely intent on pleasure. Lord Elgin's enemies afterwards described the treaty as " floated through on champagne." " Without altogether admitting this, there can be no doubt," Laurence says, " that in the hands of a skilful diplomatist that liquor is not without its value." The ambassador had been informed that if he could overcome the opposition of the Democrats, which party had a majority in the Senate, he would find no difficulty on the part of the Government. But the young secretary, keen as was his intelligence, did not see his way at first through the feasting and the gaiety into which his chief plunged. " At last, after several days of uninterrupted festivity, I began to perceive what we were driving at. To make quite sure, I said one day to my chief, ' I find all

my most intimate friends are Democratic senators.' 'So do I,' he replied, drily." This was the
young man's first lesson in statecraft. The story
of the expedition, as it more immediately concerned himself, was communicated to his parents
in a series of long letters, beginning with the
approach to Washington :—

"We never went through a tunnel the whole
journey, and were therefore well able to see
the country. When we came to towns we
went slap down the main streets, there being
nothing to keep little children from playing
upon the rails, except 'Look out for the loco-
motive' stuck up on boards. When we get
to the middle of the town we stop before the
principal hotel, and steps are put up for us as if
we were a coach changing horses. The houses
are shaded by fine old trees, and telegraph wires
run overhead in every direction, like bridges from
one cocoa-nut tree to another in Ceylon. Niggers
become plentiful as we get South, and we have
had three experiences of waiters in hotels. At the
Clarendon there was not a man at all. We were
waited on entirely by rather pretty bare-armed
maidens in a becoming and uniform costume ;
remarkably agreeable I thought it. They used to
be very attentive to me at dinner, as they saw I

appreciated their charms. There were at least fifty waiting every day. Then at the St Nicholas we had regular civilised waiters—I am afraid to say how many—but everything is done at the same moment, and there is a procession of full and empty dishes which takes about five minutes to complete itself. Then at Philadelphia all the waiters were niggers, and now we are in the land of Æthiopian serenaders. We reached Philadelphia about twelve o'clock. The scenery as we approached became very pretty, the rail passed along the banks of the broad Delaware, fringed with bright foliage to the water's edge, and clothed with islands. The wood is all of comparatively young growth; but the country is often charmingly diversified. Philadelphia is the second city in the Union, and the handsomest. The broad streets lined with trees, the shady squares, the massive white marble houses, all add to its imposing appearance. We only stayed there an hour, and then went to a terminus or depôt, as it is called, at the other end of the town. For day travelling the American cars are very convenient: they are always full of pretty girls, and if the scenery is not pretty you can look at them,—they are always sure to be looking at you. In the same carriage with us we had that notorious Irish "patriot" John Mitchell, another editor of a paper, a very disreputable-looking blackguard, and Routledge the cheap publisher, an intelligent, pushing fellow, who is come over to spy out the nakedness of the land, and is going to set up a shop in the States and Canada, and beat the Yankees on their own ground."

Passing on through Maryland, the first slave State, they spent an hour at Baltimore, which is described as being "more full of niggers and less of trees than the others we had seen" : this time was occupied in visiting the Roman Catholic cathedral. They then proceeded by train to Washington, where they arrived late in the evening. After dinner they were "energetic enough to go at once to the Capitol to see the final vote taken on the Nebraska Bill, a measure which has caused more sensation, and is likely to lead to more important results, than any which has ever come before Congress."

"Considering, however, the tone of the papers, there was not so much excitement manifested as I had anticipated. The whole place was crowded, the galleries full of ladies, and when the bill in favour of slavery was carried by 100 to 113, the cheering was considerable. It is likely to lead to totally new combinations of parties, and the candidates at the next election will go to the country upon the question of slavery or abolition. It may possibly," he goes on, "lead to a revolution, so strong is the feeling on both sides. Members have come to Congress every night armed to the teeth, and it is quite an accident that there has not been a row : however, it is all over for the present, and there is a lull, during which we hope to effect our little plans. I was rather disappointed at there not being a row, and only two honourable members were drunk. One was obliged to be carried out, but did not show any sport ; the other asked me what the fools were voting about : considering the row there was at the time, I should not have been surprised at the question even had he been sober."

Laurence found the hotel at Washington uncomfortable, and the aspect of the place depressing, consisting of a wide long avenue, with the Capitol at one end and the President's house at the other. In fact, as he says of it, " it is a town without a population, and exists only by virtue of its being the seat of Government." He found his time also a good deal taken up, not with actual official work, but with much moving about, in constant attendance on Lord Elgin. The

Queen's Birthday, however, broke the monotony a little.

"There was a grand flare - up at Crampton's, at which all the beauty and fashion of Washington were assembled. There were numbers of pretty girls, who were delighted at getting hold of Mr Oliphant, 'the traveller,' for by that term I am always introduced, and I found it difficult to be free and easy enough to please them. For instance, one carried me off to a quiet bench in the garden, and because I did not sit down, but stood respectfully talking, she got up, saying, 'Well, if you won't sit down alongside of me, it's no use my sitting here all night.' I need not say that after such an invitation I exerted myself in a way which won her affections 'slick off.' Notwithstanding which, I was rather astonished when, being seduced by her into a waltz, the only one in which I indulged, a fellow came up and took 'a twist with my gal.' I asked whether that was the custom, and was assured that I had nothing to complain of. Another girl whom I took in to supper asked for ice, so I gave her some, and could only find a fork, which I handed to her, on which she said, 'Fancy eating ice with a fork!' However, I paid her off by handing her a huge table-knife, and pointing in justification to a lady who was ladling in cream in a way frightfully dangerous to behold. Most of the young ladies I was introduced to asked me to call upon them. Yesterday we had a great day in the Senate, and there is to be some serious squabbling there to-day, which I am going up with Lord E. to hear."

The interesting part of American politics at this time would appear to have been the "rows"; and diplomatic work with Lord Elgin could not have been very fatiguing, since, as he says, they were engaged every night for a week, and "the serious business of our visit is not yet in train." Laurence, however, entertained no doubt of his own diplomatic abilities when they should be called for.

"I have been engaged making arrangements for interviews with Ministers all the morning, and my diplomatic powers are considerably in request, as they are 'cute dodgy fellows, and have always got a sinister motive in the background, which it is sometimes difficult to discover. To-morrow, I suppose, we shall be hard at it : 1 shall be delighted. At the same time, this is a most relaxing and depressing place, close muggy air — Kandy temperature exactly — and streets silent and lifeless. The last place in the world, notwithstanding the pretty girls, that I should choose as a residence. I am going to join their riding-parties if I have time, and will get to know them 'to their middle initials,' the height of Yankee intimacy."

The next letter, also from Washington, is dated the 28th May, and, stimulated by the receipt of a letter from his mother, is full of grave personal subjects. He finds himself in a difficult position, delighted and grateful for the expression of her increased confidence in him, and her joy at the proofs she receives of his changed and improved character; but at the time tormented by the thought that while he would not by throwing doubt on these proofs take away any of her consolation, he could not persuade himself that, though he was a little the better for his experience, there was any real cause for self-gratulation.

"My experience," he says, "has always been very slow indeed, and while I recognise that an important change has been going on in my sentiments upon many things, still I feel as much embarrassed and perplexed as I ever did. Not that I am rendered in any way so miserable as I used to be, nor that I ever experience those violent revulsions of feeling; but wherever there is a struggle there must be times of depression. It is a merciful thing that I take very little pleasure in that gaiety in which I am obliged to mix, and by which formerly I should have been intoxicated. And perhaps the pleasure of life seems much diminished by the reflection that one must be in a dangerous condition if one is not sacrificing some favourite passion, however much it may be changed by the progress of time, &c., &c. I heard this morning an admirable sermon, and one which was peculiarly applicable to me, in answer to my desire that I should hear something to stimulate to more vigorous resistance—upon 'one thing thou lackest.' My difficulty is to realise divine things sufficiently to encourage me. The strongest incentive I have to follow my convictions upon such subjects is the inward peace and comfort which doing so has always brought to me, and the opposite effect of indulging myself. Therefore upon the lowest grounds I am disposed to practise self-denial. In my present capacity I am not engaged in any work of benevolence or charity by which I could, as it were, support myself. And though, no doubt, by my example I might glorify God, it is a much more difficult matter to do so in a ball-room at the French ambassador's, surrounded by as unthinking a throng as ever tripped the light fantastic, than down in Westminster surrounded by M'Gregor, Fowler, & Co. At the same time, I never saw more clearly the possibility of living in the world and not being of it. At present I am as satisfied that it is my duty to go to balls as to go to the Sunday-school was, provided I go in a right spirit; but it is easy to theorise. Perhaps I shall have an opportunity of testing my resolution in a very simple matter, about which nevertheless you have often expressed yourself—the matter of champagne. In Edinburgh I did not think it worth the sacrifice; but, as is often the case, one is forced into a line of conduct by the additional force of the temptation. It was only this morning that I felt the duty of putting the restraint upon myself of total abstinence, from my yesterday's experience, which was as follows:—

"At two o'clock our whole party went to a grand luncheon at a senator's. Here we had every sort of refreshing luxury, the day being pipingly hot, and dozens of champagne were polished off. Several senators got screwed, and we made good use of the two hours we had to spare before going to the French ambassador's *matinée dansante* at four. Here the same thing went on, with the addition of a lot of pretty girls whom I had before met, and who bullied one to dance, and were disgusted if you did not flirt with them. Everybody drinks champagne here, and there was a bowl on the table in which you might have drowned a baby, of most delicious and insinuating concoction. Then there were gardens, and bouquets, and ices, and strawberries, and bright eyes till six, when we had to rush off and dress for a grand dinner at a governor's. Here we had a magnificent repast. The old story of champagne, besides a most elaborate and highly got up French-cookery dinner, lasting from seven till ten, when we left the table, having been eating and drinking without intermission since two. We then adjourned with a lot of senators to brandy-and-water, champagne, and cigars till twelve, when some of us were quite ready to tumble into bed. Now I have no doubt you are perfectly horrified, and picture to yourself your inebriated son going to bed in a condition you never thought possible; but, on the contrary, yesterday was a most profitable day to me. In the first place, though I did not restrain myself, I did not in the slightest degree exceed. I did not touch anything else *but* champagne, and stopped exactly at the right moment. I felt all through that I was in a position not of my own seeking, and that if it was agreeable to me it was because I myself was at fault. I felt that it was only not positively disgusting because I participated, and that if I had not touched a thing I could not but have been excessively bored. I have therefore resolved never to touch another drop of champagne while in Washington, not because I took too much, but because I see that whether I am doing right or wrong depends entirely upon the spirit in which I participate in these things. It is necessary to the success of our mission that we conciliate everybody, and to refuse their invitations would be considered insulting. Lord Elgin pretends to drink immensely, but I watched him, and I don't believe he drank a glass between two and twelve. He is the most thorough *diplomat* possible,—never loses sight for a moment of his object, and while he is chaffing Yankees and slapping them on the back, he is systematically pursuing that object. The consequence is, he is the most popular Englishman that ever visited the United States. If you have got to deal with hogs, what are you to do? As Canning said of a man, 'He goes the whole hog, and he looks the hog he goes,' which is precisely a description of this respectable race; but I have no occasion even to pretend to drink their wine, and I shall therefore not do it. I was perfectly well this morning, but Sir Cusack Roney and Hincks are both laid up—poor Sir Q., as we call him, fairly knocked up, or rather down, by such unaccustomed proceedings. As I said, I am so far grateful to it all if it is the means of making me form resolutions and sticking to them, which less prominent dissipation, such as that of Edinburgh, would never have done.

" But a far more difficult matter than the champagne is the young ladies. My natural temperament not being amorous but very joyous, I get too boisterous, or rather reckless, in flirting, for simple fun. Therefore, though there is no absolute command against other than idle words, which is one none of us can very strictly apply, yet I feel that I have been talking an amount of nonsense of which my conscience is ashamed, and the effect of a whole afternoon spent in the way I have described, which would formerly be to distract and unsettle me, has been to sober and solemnise me, and to make me think how I am to meet the difficulties opposed to me. Under other circumstances, I should keep away from the drinking—this would be no sacrifice; from the ladies it would be one that I could easily make. I should call upon the missionaries if I was going to live here, and employ myself as I did in London ; but I am called upon to join in everything, and my conscience would not in the slightest degree twit me for doing so, provided I was all the time bored instead of pleased. The test of the thing is whether I like it, and though I cannot say I do, I very soon would, and therefore it is I must be especially watchful, while it would be comparatively easy for me to form and keep resolutions: and I have enjoyed the quiet of to-day and the sermon, which was very comforting, though it inculcated a serious lesson. I am glad you spoke about the tobacco, but at present there is no fear of that; Lord Elgin hates smoking, and I do not like it in this jovial soil of parties. I have not smoked half-a-dozen cigars since leaving England, and every one has been a solitary one, when I wanted to compose myself and think. I think it prostitutes tobacco to drink and talk over it. However, I shall never care really about it, and it is very seldom that I am in the humour— generally when I am disgusted with myself; and I am more self-satisfied, or to speak more truly, have more tranquillity than I used to have, and do not need soothing. Your letter was worth all the cigars in the world."

After what he himself termed "this long confession," the letter turned to business. He had received much applause in America on the subject of his book, and had begun to inquire within himself whether he could write a book which he felt ought to be written—namely, a philosophical treatise on the American constitution, with the chief heads of " slavery, federalism, and the great questions upon which, sooner or later, the Union must fall to pieces." This, by the way, in 1854, was not a bad prophecy for a young man, who had not been in the country a month. " The fallacies of the form of government," he says, " are only dawning on me, and I should require a long course of reading and observation before entering upon so serious a task ; but it would be the most interesting topic possible, and one which, when it does force itself upon public attention, will engross the whole world." Right as he was in some of his prognostics, he had no time to give to this work, though he left the subject with a whimsical regret, " It would be a great thing to have another book out in the nick of time."

One more letter which followed from Washington was filled with a sort of chronicle of the days between 31st May and 5th June. He had at last got to work, though it was while waiting for Lord Elgin to give him something to do that he took the opportunity of writing his letter.

" I was occupied the greater part of yesterday in writing officially. I am afraid I make a bad secretary : my forte does not lie in business matters. In fact, I should be the head of the department, not the clerk. It is so fearfully hot and relaxing that one is not disposed for hard work. I have not much new to tell. We dine out as usual, and the dinners last three hours as usual, and I generally get between two senators, one of whom pours abolitionism in my ear, the other, the divine origin of slavery. The politics of this country are most complicated, and difficult to understand ; there are so many different parties, rejoicing in so many different names. There are the Whigs, and Democrats, and Filibusters, and Hard Shells, and Soft Shells, and Free-Soilers, and Disunionists, and Federalists,—all of whom expect you to understand at once their distinctive characteristics. I have not time to 'post myself' up in all these matters, nor to see sights—in fact, America would be a great deal more difficult to write about than Russia, its constitution being so much more complicated, and its practical working so very different from its theory."

This conclusion, however, does not hinder him from indicating his opinion on various points : as, for instance, that whereas the President should be one of the first men in the country, he was in fact, as a rule, a mere cipher in point of intellect ; and that bribery and corruption prevailed as universally as in Russia, though in a different way. Many American writers, in days since Laurence's letters were written, have pointed out this tendency and opening to corruption as the great inherent fault in their constitution. To investigate such a serious question, however, so as to find out its real cause, required more time than Laurence could give to it, as " now that Colonel Bruce, and Sir Cusack and Lady Roney have gone, and Hamilton is laid up in New York," he remained the only companion of Lord Elgin, and could go nowhere on his own account; so that he would seem to have given up the idea of writing a book.

"There is a great deal of self-denial involved with the conscientious discharge of my duties, and I am obliged to decline invitations to riding-parties, &c., &c., and take a sober stroll instead— all very good discipline, no doubt. It is a very great advantage to me, being behind the scenes in a matter of this kind, and seeing how an able man like Lord E. manages affairs. I compare him with papa. They have a good many points of similarity in their way of venting their indignation and fuming, and yet never acting impulsively. I occasionally take a look in upon Bury, who is living in another hotel : it is

pleasant to look upon a kent face. I think it
very possible that, now that Colonel Bruce has
left Canada, I may act as Lord Elgin's private
secretary there.   However, that is only a suppo-
sition on my part : nothing has been said to me
about it, so don't mention it; of course I should
be glad to be employed in any way. . . . I am
keeping all the accounts, and I think there must
be a mistake somewhere, as I have expended and
received some hundreds of dollars, and they come
right exactly, which is most strange and unexpected.

"The other night I was dining out with rather
a singular houseful of people : the master of the
house was a senator, a methodist preacher, and a
teetotaller ; consequently, although it was a party
of twenty people, we had nothing to drink but iced
water.   His wife, who unfortunately was not there,
is a spirit medium, and in constant communication
with the nether, though she calls it the upper, world.
Her daughter, who sat next me at dinner, is a
Bloomer, and never wears any other costume ; she
has an ugly shambling figure, and cuts the most
absurd appearance : her husband is an avowed and
rampant infidel, so that altogether it was a very
odd if not instructive assemblage.   I don't know
how they all manage to get on together.   For the
preacher must look upon his son-in-law as a viper,

and the son-in-law must look upon his mother as
an impostor, and they must all look upon his wife
as a fool—while she takes very good care to show
the world that she wears the breeches."

Many other amusing notes follow as to the
people he meets. On one occasion the gentleman
sitting next him volunteered the information that
he (the speaker) was a singular man, and related
his history ; how, left without a farthing at seven
years old, he managed to pay for his own education out of his earnings, qualified as a barrister
at the age of twenty-one, being then the proud
owner of just 2 dollars 50 cents in the world, and
owing 500 dollars ; how, being not yet thirty, he
had already lost wife and child, and was looking
out for another bride to go with him on a journey
to Europe, to study the politics of other countries
before he came back to embark upon a political
career in his own. On the morning of the day
on which Laurence wrote, his companions were
of a still more remarkable kind.

"On one side of me was the governor of the
new Territory of Washington, which lies to the
north of Oregon, upon the North Pacific, and is
seventy days' journey from this place : on the
other side was a senator from Florida, who gave

me some curious information about those parts. Then I made great friends with the celebrated Colonel Fremont, who is a splendid fellow, and has been more nearly starved to death, and more often in that predicament, 'than any other man in creation, don't care where you look for him.' Then there was Colonel Benton, who is writing a great work, and is 'quite a fine man'; and Mr Senator Toombs, who is to be president some of these days; and the governor of Wisconsin, whose government has increased in population, within ten years, from 30,000 to 500,000, and who met a man the other day who had travelled over the whole globe, and examined it narrowly with an eye to agricultural capabilities, and who therefore was an authority not to be disputed; and this man said that he had never, in any country, seen fifty square miles to equal that extent in the State of Wisconsin, and therefore it was quite clear that the spot was not contained in creation. As other provincials have informed me that their respective States are each thus singularly gifted, I am beginning to get puzzled as to which really is indisputably the most fertile spot on the face of the habitable globe.

"I have every hope that we shall polish off our treaty to-morrow, in which case we shall retire in the evening, covered with glory. It is a most exciting operation, and for the last few days, as matters have approached a crisis, I have been at it from morning till night, and then dreaming about it. The alternation of hope and fear is most trying, as new difficulties are suggested, and methods of solving them proposed, and new concessions gained, and the old Secretary of State bamboozled. Hincks goes away to-day, and Lord Elgin and I will be left alone. There are so many fellows opposed to the treaty, and so much underworking, that it requires considerable 'cuteness and caution to manage matters; but Lord Elgin is a match for them, and it is a pleasure to see how he works the matter. It would be of advantage to a fool, and of course it is invaluable to a clever cove like me, who is given to appropriating other men's dodges."

While all this serious and exciting business was proceeding, the dinners and *matinées dansantes* seem also to have gone on as continuously as ever, and " the soft balmy evenings in pretty gardens, with fruits and ices, and ' quite a clever piece ' for a companion, are enjoyable enough." The next letter is dated the 7th of June, the last having ended on the 5th, and was written at New York, where he had arrived after the successful issue of the negotiations at Washington.

" We are tremendously triumphant ; we have signed a stunning treaty. When I say we, it was in the dead of night, in the last five minutes of the 5th of June, and the first five minutes of the 6th day of the month aforesaid, that in a spacious chamber, by the brilliant light of six wax-candles and an argand, four individuals might have been observed seated, their faces expressive of deep and earnest thought, not unmixed with cunning. Their feelings, however, to the acute observer manifested themselves in different ways ; and this was but natural, as two were young and two aged,—one, indeed, far gone in years, the other prematurely so. He it is whose measured tones alone break the solemn silence of midnight, except when one of the younger auditors, who are intently poring over voluminous MSS., interrupts him to interpolate ' and ' or scratch out ' the.' They are, in fact, checking him ; and the aged man listens while he picks his teeth with a pair of scissors, or clears out the wick of the candle with their points and wipes them on his hair. He may occasionally be observed to wink, either from conscious 'cuteness or unconscious drowsiness. Attached to these three MSS. by red ribbon are the heavy seals. Presently the clock strikes twelve, and there is a doubt whether to date it to-day or yesterday. For a

moment there is a solemn silence, and he who
was reading takes the pen, which has previously
been impressively dipped in the ink by the most
intelligent of the young men, who appears to be
his secretary, and who keeps his eye warily upon
the other young man, who is the opposition secretary, and interesting as a specimen of a Yankee
in that capacity. There is something strangely
mysterious in the scratching. of that midnight
pen, for it is scratching away the destinies of
nations; and then it is placed in the hands of
the venerable file, whose hand does not shake,
though he is very old, and knows he will be
bullied to death by half the members of Congress. The hand that has used a revolver upon
previous similar occasions does not waver with
a pen, though the lines he traces may be an
involver of a revolver again. He is now the
Secretary of State; before that, he was a judge
of the Supreme Court; before that, a general in
the army; before that, governor of a State; before
that, Secretary at War; before that, minister in
Mexico; before that, a member of the House of
Representatives; before that, an adventurer; before that, a cabinet-maker. So why should the
old man fear? Has he not survived the changes
and chances of more different sorts of lives than
any other man? and is he afraid of being done

by an English lord? So he gives us his blessing, and we leave the old man and his secretary with our treaty in our pockets."

This letter was finished at Boston in the middle of the continued journey. Laurence had been sent on at once to New York, where he was kept awake all night by a demonstration in favour of a senator in the same hotel, so that the vigil consequent upon the completion of the treaty was not his only one. After this he travelled on " through lovely country, wooded and watered and smiling, up glens in the railway, which in these countries prefers going up and down hill to going through tunnels, and going past lakes embedded in foliage, with pretty villages of white wooden houses inhabited by prim descendants of the Pilgrim Fathers—and so on to this city, more like an English commercial emporium than any other in the States; and to-morrow we undergo a grand triumphal reception at Portland, and next day another at Montreal, and next day another at Quebec, all which I hope to find time to tell you of in my next. Meanwhile Lord Elgin is rejoicing in the prospect of about six speeches a-day, and I in hopes of amusing myself, which, indeed, I have been doing very fairly all along. We have got Sir Cu. and Lady Roney, and in addition to them a Sir Henry and Lady Caldwell, in our party."

The details of description which he continues to give us he passes along may be less interesting to the sophisticated reader, who since then has heard so much of America; but they are at least brief and graphic. Portland, where the party "arrived under a salute, and went in procession to the house of one of the leading citizens," Laurence described as "lovely." "The situation of Portland is very striking, on a high promontory which overlooks an immense bay, on which upwards of three hundred islands are dotted; while towards the interior a richly wooded and fertile country stretches away to the base of the White Mountains, 6000 feet high. The town is well laid out—every street an avenue of noble trees, and the houses substantially built. It is destined before long to rival Boston, and will form the main outlet for Canadian produce. This treaty will be the making of it; and the inhabitants no doubt felt that they could not sufficiently honour the man who had done more for their town than anybody else."

The festivities here consisted chiefly of a great banquet, at which "Lord Elgin delighted them with his happy speeches"; and "I distinguished myself in responding to a 'sentiment' of a liter-

ary character with which my name was coupled."
The entrance of the Mission into Canada after
this partook of the character of a royal progress,
with triumphal arches, cheering crowds, and welcoming speeches at all the stations. But at
Montreal, "where the population is somewhat
uncertain in its loyalty," their reception was by
no means so demonstrative—although the people
" behaved very decently" on the whole. From
Montreal a special steamer carried the party on to
Spencer Wood, the viceregal residence, of which
Laurence gives an enthusiastic description. He
writes on the verandah into which his rooms
open, "enjoying a Mediterranean air and more
than a Mediterranean view":—

"SPENCER WOOD, *June* 14, 1854.

" From the verandah extends a lawn studded
with noble trees to the edge of a steep wooded
bank, and among the trees rise the tapering
masts of ships, which look as if they were
eccentric branches. They are lying in the St
Lawrence, two miles broad, and filled with craft
of all sizes. It is at once peaceful and busy,
and I prefer it to the sea, as in an epicurean
point of view it is disturbing to see anything
like commotion; but quiet life is perfect. The
opposite bank of the St Lawrence is precipitous

and well wooded, with villages at the base, or
climbing up valleys or perched upon the edge,
and churches prominent and picturesque. When
I am tired of looking at the point of view over
this lovely scene which my window affords, I
stroll down a broad long avenue of magnificent
trees; and then, turning through a thick copse
by a winding path, I come upon a little wooded
gorge, down which a noisy brook tumbles; and
I follow that till it gets too impetuous for my
sentimental system, or for the proper construction of the path, which there comes out abruptly
upon the edge of a precipice where a summer-
house is perched, from which you can look up
and down the river for miles. In one direction
the swelling banks, of the most brilliant green,
are dotted with houses, for the whole country
is thickly inhabited; on the other, a lofty promontory is crowned with the fortifications of
Quebec, standing out into the river as if to
guard the beauties that are beyond. The bay
formed by the promontory on which I am, and
that on which the Fort stands, is filled with
wood. It is at once an island of planks and a
forest of masts; and as I lie listening to the
sound of the busy world, the songs of the sailors
and the clang of hammers, the laughter of children and the rushing of the stream, I can enjoy

kief to perfection; and I am afraid I have insensibly wasted some valuable time in allowing my senses to have the benefit of all these charms. Lord Elgin thinks I am the most romantic of authors, whereas I am rather surprised to find that I can now enjoy what I never before really appreciated, and I rejoice in the discovery of a new faculty of enjoyment and a fitting place to exercise it in. To be sure, I have had more to think about within the last few days than I ever had at any former period of my life—or at any rate, I have thought external circumstances worthy of more consideration than I am in the habit of doing. With one's sense of responsibility grows also the important reflection of its proper exercise, and I look upon moments of quiet as more necessary to fortify one to join in the racket of life, just in proportion as that racket is universal and becomes more distracting. I therefore recognise in the charms of Spencer Wood and the valley of the St Lawrence a legitimate source of comfort and support, intended for my benefit just when I most need it."

These somewhat solemn reflections, by which the young man excuses his love of loitering in a beautiful scene, are amusing enough; but the intimation at the end of his letter of the new position in which he suddenly found himself was enough to warrant the solemnity.

"My book has obtained for me all through our tour considerable notoriety, and I was immensely made of by the citizens of Portland and elsewhere. Here, too, where novelties are rare, I am an object of some curiosity, and am in consequence rather nervous at the prominence of my position —and which was so totally unexpected. I think I had just heard of it as I closed my last letter to you. Know, then, that I am now Superintendent - General of Indian Affairs, having succeeded Colonel Bruce in that office, and having as my subordinates two colonels, two captains (all of militia), and some English gentlemen who have been long in the service, and who must look rather suspiciously at the 'Oriental Traveller's' interposition. However, I hope to get on pretty well, notwithstanding I already contemplate rowing one of the colonels and turning him out if he is not more attentive to his duties."

The appointment of so young a man, not even a member of the Civil Service, and entirely new to Canada and its needs, was evidently by no means a popular one, if we may trust the cut-

tings from Canadian papers which accompany
these letters; and caused great talk of favourit-
ism, and the sacrifice of the public service to
private motives. He himself, however, was full
of great intentions on the subject, and a determination to do his duty. He writes in a sub-
sequent letter that he has not been fully employed, and is disgusted by the waste of time.

"SPENCER WOOD, *July* 7.

"However, it is not altogether lost, for I have
been revolving great projects in my brain. One
is to remodel to a great extent the Indian Department, and the whole system upon which the
Indian tribes are at present managed. However,
it must be done with caution and well matured, as
I suspect the Government will not readily assent
to my views, which are a little arbitrary and des-
potic. Then I am going to compile information
for a book which I have been planning. It is to
be a sort of treatise on constitutional government,
contrasting this country with the United States,
showing the abuses of the latter and the advantages of responsible government. I have got
such great advantages here in the way of material, that I do not like to let the opportunity slip.
At the same time, it is such a tremendous undertaking, and I commence it in a condition of such

abject ignorance, that I have not as yet plucked up courage to face it. Moreover, it is a nervous operation to risk one's reputation upon so grand a theme. However, success will be all the more glorious, and I shall not be in a hurry, but digest and compile slowly; and then, when the great crash comes in the States which is inevitable, I will try and turn out a few notions on the crisis at the nick of time. If the crisis does not come, I shall put my information into an anonymous form, rather than publish anything with my name that is not paramountly interesting. If Aunt M. and others wish to know whether my appointment is permanent, pray say that I am most thankful it is not. Nothing can be a greater curse to a young man wishing to get on than a permanent appointment. It is certainly not the quickest way to get up a ladder to establish one's self on the lowest step."

And here is a piece of precocious youthful wisdom, perhaps not quite so wise as that above quoted. It is given with the absolute certainty which members of the human race possess at twenty-five. "No man who has been the editor of a Government paper for twenty years can retain his honesty. You see how the 'Times' has been obliged to go into opposition : they were

losing their influence fast. Nothing is more established than the fact that the newspaper which
exerts the greatest influence in a country must
be in opposition. It is also sure of a larger cir-
culation, because Government supporters are obliged to take it to see what is said, and the
opponents take it because they agree with it.

"I confess," adds the young man, going back
to questions less abstract, "that I am rather fas-
cinated with the new world. There is such
scope for great political chances and changes.
Now that we have got reciprocity, there can be
no doubt that Canada is best off as she is, in spite
of all the nonsense that ass Ellenborough talked.
It is a great comfort to feel that if the old world
does not pay we can fall back upon the new.
There is plenty of room, and great facilities for
becoming rich."

Another letter, however, from the paradise of
Spencer Wood, where his mind was full of so
many projects, both practical and visionary, is
of a very different tone. It is like the opening
of a door in the secret chamber of the young
man's heart and thoughts, at which his mother
was continually knocking, anxious above all
things to know how his mind stood in respect
to the momentous matters of religion, in which,
from his earliest childhood, she had desired con-

tinual confidences. I do not know what Lady Oliphant's distinctive views were at this time. They were, perhaps, a little open to the influence of the prevailing preacher who interested and instructed her; but they were always full of profound and emotional piety, and her strongest desire was that her son should be like herself, placing sacred subjects in absolute pre-eminence both in his thoughts and life—and that he should tell her so. He writes on a Sunday morning, when "kept back by a wet day from going to church."

"SPENCER WOOD, *July* 9.

"Just now, however, the sun has burst forth from behind the clouds, and makes nature here look more lovely than ever. While enjoying it just now, I was struck with the congenial sentiments expressed in the Psalm to which I was referred in Bogatsky, the 143d : they seemed exactly to explain my feelings. The more sensible one is of the magnificence of the works of creation, the more incompetent one feels to live worthily of the author of them, and a sort of feeling of desolation is induced, which David evidently sympathised with. There is a hopeless longing to be assimilated to the Creator, no doubt increasing in intensity in proportion as one appreciates His works ; and in spite of any combinations of external circumstances which, so far as the world is concerned, seem enough to make one perfectly happy and contented, the very fact of one's being capable of a certain degree of enjoyment makes one desire a still higher order. Of nothing am I more certain than of the incompetency of any earthly gratification affording happiness just on the same principle : it is always accompanied with an indefinable longing for something more, just as when one contemplates nature and enjoys it most keenly, the soul begins to thirst after God as a thirsty land, and 'the heart within is desolate.' David evidently looked upon nature as an appointed means of elevating the soul. So many of his aspirations have their origin in this; and in admiring God's works nothing can be more natural than an ardent desire to be imbued as largely as possible with the same spirit that breathes in them. 'Thy spirit is good.' As I think I said in a letter some time ago, we do not half appreciate the influence of the Spirit. I am perhaps inclined to give it too prominent a place, my natural inclination being to overlook the Second Person as the only recognised means of obtaining the Third. But that is just where my faith is most severely tried. Everything around me testifies to the existence of a Being who is all-pervading; but the Son is nowhere visible, and does not, so to speak, force Himself upon the senses. It is a totally different act of the mind which is required to accept Him as a positive fact. To speak in old Erskine's phraseology, the subjective Tally is wanting, which, in the Deity and His Spirit, as manifested in nature, is so readily found. However, I have rather wandered from the original idea, which presented itself forcibly on reading the Psalm; and it is worthy of observation that David had not only the subjective as regards God in nature but in Christ, and that by an act of faith infinitely more difficult than ours, as it was prospective. This want on my part is therefore the result, doubtless, of a small measure of the Spirit, and I have the most perfect confidence that if I earnestly desire to be taught and confirmed on this point, the Spirit will effectually operate. At present, with the small measure I as yet possess, and the pertinacity with which I grieve and offend it in spite of its remonstrances, I can scarcely expect to make any rapid progress; but I think you will understand from what I have said how the 143d Psalm should chime in with my feelings, and be comforting in showing how a man of David's spirituality was occasionally led to lament over his own weakness while meditating on God's works. You used to say that the more

I was favoured by external circumstances, the more I grumble and am discontented with myself. I think even after David was a king he was occasionally affected in like manner, and were it not so, one would be disposed to think that one was deserted altogether, and left to one's own evil devices."

While thus, however, opening his heart to his mother in the way she most eagerly desired, he was very anxious not to give her too high an idea of his spiritual progress, or represent himself as better than he felt himself to be; and in the end of the same letter, continued some days later, he protests against her too delighted reception of such spiritual confidences.

"I think you overrate my progress, and give way to your natural impulses too much in the expression of such ardent rejoicings. I only hope they will not be turned into mourning. I am of course very glad of anything that reconciles you to our separation; but at the same time feel my own weakness too much to desire that you should repose too much confidence in my resolutions, or anticipate too great results from what I wrote. This is just one of the reasons which make me hesitate about expressing so very much. It would be far better for you not to form extravagant expectations, than having formed them to be disappointed. However, I do not mean that you should not be grateful with all humility, or that it is not natural, if you feel comforted during my absence, that you should say so; only you must remember that the effects of it might be to produce a spirit of self-satisfaction in me, or a desire to write more of the same comfortable doctrine when I don't feel it, with many other bad effects—to say nothing of the dreadful reaction which is always possible, and which is indeed inevitable when any one emotion is allowed an undue influence. There is a most ungrateful lecture to return to such an affecting outpouring as few sons, I am sure, ever received; but however agreeable it may have been at the time, the danger of going to extremes in these matters struck me too forcibly not to make me feel warranted in telling you, as you always ask me to do so."

The important post to which he had been appointed, and which carried him into untrodden ways, and put the affairs of the Canadian Red men into his youthful keeping, with no experience, and only his native intelligence, shrewdness, and keen perception of human character to guide him, gave him material for an interesting and amusing book, 'Minnesota and the Far West,' published immediately after his return, and for some further recollections published in the 'Episodes in a Life of Adventure,' which make it unnecessary to enter largely into them here. In the carrying out of this work, he had to travel far into the depths of the country, and to meet with many novel experiences. "This duty," he says, "was eminently to my taste. It involved diving into the depths of the backwoods, bark-canoeing on distant and silent lakes or down foaming rivers, where the fishing was splendid, the scenery most romantic, and camp-life at this season of the year, for it was the height of summer, most enjoyable." It was a prolonged picnic, with just enough duty thrown in to deprive it of any character of selfishness. At nearly all the stations there was a school or mission-house of some kind, and here the meeting of the warriors and young braves with their "father" (himself) took place, —"and as I had barely attained the age of twenty-five when these paternal responsibilities were thrust upon me, the incongruity of my relation towards them, I am afraid, presented itself somewhat forcibly to the minds of the veterans on these occasions." The most important result of his work among them seems to have been, as in the case of the work in Washington, the signing of a treaty. Two State negotiations more different than that between Great Britain and the United States, and that by which the poor Indians gave up for a substantial consideration the land previously allotted to them, but which their wandering habits prevented them from making any proper use of, could scarcely be. But the young diplomatist found interest in both.

The latter part of Lord Elgin's viceroyalty was full of stirring Colonial politics, changes of Ministry and much political commotion; and when the young Superintendent of Indian Affairs returned to Quebec from his voyage to the West, it was to resume the duties of his Excellency's private secretary in troubled times — the trouble, however, doing little more than add a zest to the work, and a little excitement to life. "My position here is very agreeable," he writes; "I have pleasant alternatives of excitement and tranquillity, always plenty to occupy me, a climate which agrees with me better than any other I ever was in; and in many ways I think I am gaining much valuable experience.

"I found no less than ten official letters, besides the English mail, awaiting me this morning. I had moreover four appointments of gentlemen wanting interviews, a lot of incidental coves to stave off from his Excellency, which I flatter myself is the part of the business I excel in most. They always leave infinitely better pleased than if they had had their interview. My life is much like that of a Cabinet Minister or Parliamentary swell, now that the House is sitting. I am there every night till the small hours, taking little relaxations in the shape of evening visits when a bore gets up. That keeps me in bed till late, so that breakfast and the drive in (from Spencer Wood), &c., detain me from the office till near one. Then I get through business for the next three hours—chiefly consisting of drafting letters, which in the end I ought to be a dab at. I have three bell-ropes hanging at my right hand communicating with my two departments and the messengers. I also append my valuable signature to a great deal without knowing in the least why, and run out to the most notorious gossips to pick up the last bits of news, political or social, with which to regale his Excellency, who duly rings for me for that purpose when he has read his letters and had his interviews. Then he walks out with an A.D.C., and I go to the House. There I take up my seat on a chair exclusively my own next the Speaker, and members (I have made it my business to know them nearly all) come and tell me the news, and I am on chaffing terms with the Opposition, and on confidential with the Ministerialists. If I see pretty girls in the galleries who are friends of mine (the galleries are always full), I go up there and criticise members and draw caricatures of them, which they throw down into members' laps neatly folded, who pass them to the original,—by which time I have regained my seat, and the demure secretary remains profoundly political and unsuspected. I find nothing so difficult as keeping up my dignity, and when the Bishop or a Cabinet Minister calls, I take their apologies for intruding as if I was doing them a favour. I am afraid of hazarding a joke unless I am quite sure it is a good one. I suppose the dignity of the office was so well sustained by Bruce, that they are scandalised by a larky young cove like me."

More serious matters, however, mingled with the fun with which the gay young secretary diversified his life. On the day after a great picnic, terminating in an impromptu dance which was his suggestion, and which accordingly he devoted all his faculties to carry out successfully, he describes himself as "fairly done up."

" The Ministers were determined to push through the answer" (to the Governor's speech from the throne), " in order that by large majorities they might influence the election of the new Ministers in Upper Canada; the Opposition were determined to defeat that object: so it was a question of who would sit it out. The consequence was a debate of twenty-two hours. I had dined out and gone to an evening party, and then went to the House and remained till half-past four, when Mackenzie the quondam rebel got up to make a rambling speech which I hear lasted for four hours; but I left, and when I returned at one in the afternoon I found the House still sitting, so you see Parliament is not a mere sham in this country, and its value is properly appreciated. On Thursday we had a succession of grand doings, beginning at twelve, accounts of which you will see in the papers. Lord Elgin made a magnificent oration in French: it is really a pleasure to be attached to such a man, so stunning in certain respects. It created a great sensation. The whole thing was novel and exciting: first the reception by a dozen purple episcopates in the Archbishop's palace, and then the opening of a Roman Catholic college by his Excellency. Your liberality would not quite come such a stretch as that. There

were some thousands of people assembled. Some
of the Protestants here are highly disgusted, but
I highly approve. No sooner was this proceeding over than we received the dutiful answer to
the address from the Commons, which was an echo
of the Governor's speech, and a great triumph
to him after all the abuse that has been lavished
upon him. The answer has been carried through
the House by overwhelming majorities. After
that we received a quantity more of purple
ecclesiastics. All this time I had been in full
dress, white tie, &c. Then to the House till
dinner, when I dined with Mr Primrose, Lord
Rosebery's brother, who afterwards had a ball,
where I remained till pretty late. Not the best
preparation in the world for our own ball at
Spencer Wood to-night; but I shall cut some of
that by staying in the House to see the Reciprocity Treaty through. It was read last night for
the first time. However, the Governor says the
success of the ball depends upon me. I have introduced four new dances into Quebec. What
an enviable reputation to have, and how astonished my Edinburgh friends would be! and yet
I don't care nearly so much for gaiety as I used
to do. Only whatever I undertake I like to
carry out with a will; and if we are to leave
Canada with a flare-up after eight years of the

most successful administration that any Governor
ever had, I will do my best."

"Society here is really very agreeable," he
adds. "There are no sets or jealousies, but
everybody is on excellent terms and very good-
natured." As usual, he was specially interested
in one portion of society. I do not know if the
peculiar institution hereafter described has found
a place in any other record : "The girls are for
the most part lively and pretty, with a deal of
French in them, which prevents their having a
taste for solid information, but makes up for it by
giving them plenty of small talk and fascinating
manners. I go upon the principle of dispensing
my favours so liberally that my attentions cannot
be said to be particular, though that is not at all
the fashion. Every girl has what is called her
muffin,—some *devoué*, who never leaves her side,
dances with her always when he is not sitting
with her in a dark corner, and behaves as if he
were engaged. This, however, is not the case,
nor is it expected. It is quite an understood
thing that he is her muffin and she his, not her
future husband, and curiously enough no harm
ever comes of it. Sometimes it ends in marriage,
but never in anything else."

There is a great deal about these young ladies

in the letters, especially as his time draws towards
an end; and he becomes full of questions as to
his conduct,—whether he has kept up to his own
standard, whether it would be possible for him to
keep up to it if he stayed longer, and how his
young successor, with whom he has had many
confidences on the subject of religion — sometimes feeling that his advices do the young man
good, sometimes that his inconsistencies do him
harm—will be able to withstand the many tempta-
tions of society.   For Quebec society, with that
delightful mixture of French ease and lightness,
with the charms and frankness of the ladies, the
good-humour and freedom and friendliness of all
around, is sadly against serious thought : and as
he half impels and half is impelled by his chief
into the blaze of entertainment and gaiety which
is wanted to make a brilliant conclusion to Lord
Elgin's administration, his doubts and tribulations
grow more and more.   " Lord E. says he never
knows what I am at, at one moment going to the
extreme of gaiety, at another to that of disgust
and despondency.   All he wishes is in a good-
natured way to amuse people ; and he therefore
can hardly sympathise with my reactions every
now and then, which arise from my being too
well amused myself.   He sees my twinges of conscience, and asked me the other day whether I

was going to lay all the sins I seemed so much oppressed with at his door? At another he said, " All these comments of yours upon our proceedings distress me very much. After all, we are only amusing people, and if you have got anything to repent of, I wish you'd wait and do it on board ship." Then after an outcry, which is not at all intended to be humorous, " Flesh and blood can't stand the temptation of such hosts of charming girls!" the young secretary comments somewhat demurely as follows :—

" There is a class of sins which are very difficult to resist, because you cannot put your finger upon the exact point where they become sins. Now, for instance, a certain degree of intimacy with young ladies is no harm; and it is difficult to define where flirting begins, or what amount even of joking and laughing, though perfectly innocent, is not expedient, and one gets led imperceptibly on without feeling the harm that is being done to both parties until it is too late. As I told you before, I am not in any degree involved in anything : but I daresay I should be if I stayed ; or as an alternative, become more utterly heartless in those matters than I am already."

These scruples being set to rest, or at least

temporarily silenced by being put into words, he gives a most lively description of the setting in of winter, which he had much desired to see before leaving Canada—a wish which was gratified by means of various unforeseen ministerial changes which delayed Lord Elgin's departure. Describing these changes, and lamenting the disappointment to his eagerly expectant parents in consequence, he adds :—

" Meantime I am revelling in the first burst of winter and its attendant novelty. I would not have missed it for the world. My office window looks upon the Place d'Armes, a large square. On the one side is the platform overlooking the river, forming the promenade in summer ; on the other the main street, Parliament House, &c., opposite gardens. The day is mild and calm, and the snow half a foot deep. Not a wheeled vehicle is to be seen. Cabstands all sleighs, no two alike in shape. Round the Place sleighs with tandems or pairs, full of ladies muffled up in furs, with buffalo-robes streaming behind, dash about rapidly over the crisp snow, making a merry accompaniment to its crunching with their bells, the occupants looking prettier than ever. Single men dashing about in swell turn-outs, from which I must say Bury with his blood horses bears the palm. They go round and round, cut out and in, and then dash away through the Fort gates into the snow - clad country. With a pleasant companion nothing could be more exhilarating. Some of the faster young ladies are picked up by the most insinuating young men and driven *tête-à-tête*, so snug and confiding. I had a charming muffin yesterday. She is engaged to be married, so don't be alarmed. By changing every day you are quite safe. It does not do to be particular; besides, as you may suppose, the nicest won't go even with their most particular friends unless there is a picnic or a sleighing party, though why it is more correct or less dangerous then, I cannot exactly say.

" From the platform the scene is extraordinary; the river full of floes of floating ice, which collects in the bays, and surges up into fantastic masses. People cross in canoes, and when they get to a floe, the boatmen jump on it and haul the canoe over, the occupants remaining still. I watch them from the platform. The most exciting part of sleighing is turning corners. Unless you know the dodge you are sure to upset, but it is only into the snow, and no harm is done. I have not been upset yet, and always go like the wind."

One of the most pleasant things in these letters is the character—always wholly admired, not always comprehended—the remarkable figure of the chief, his Excellency, who is sometimes called, in puzzled familiarity, " a queer fish," but whose boundless ability, his skill, his command of every resource, his plans never fully expounded, gradually dawning by degrees on the young disciple's brilliant intelligence, his sympathy yet authority, come out before us in a hundred minute touches under the hand of the writer, all unconscious that he is making any such portrait in the letter he dashes off to his mother punctual as the post, before he touches his official work. It is, of course, imperfect, and in a manner accidental; but it is admirably vivid and true. I am not aware if any memoir of the late Lord Elgin has been given to the public; but if not, the letters I have quoted would afford much admirable material to assist in such a memorial.

CHAPTER V.

THE CRIMEA.

LAURENCE returned home early in 1855, to find his parents awaiting him in London. His own prospects, however, were so unsettled—the engagement with Lord Elgin terminating on the withdrawal of the latter from office, though to be renewed at a later period—that no definite home was established in London; and the family, thus reunited, would seem to have contented themselves in lodgings, now in one street, now in another,—not a very comfortable mode of life. And it is apparent that the Chief - Justice of Ceylon, accustomed to so full an existence and to occupy a very important position in his own sphere, felt himself considerably out of his element in London, where at first he had not even the comfort of a club where he could meet his old friends, these institutions being less necessities of life in those days than they are now.

And not unnaturally Laurence, after his brief but brilliant experience of public life, found it difficult to content himself without occupation and with the doubtful prospects before him. His mind returned with a bound to its former aspirations in respect to the Crimea, and to the plan he had conceived of making a diversion in the Caucasus, and thus drawing away the attention of Russia to a country which it was of so much importance to her to overawe and secure. He had declined an offer made to him to remain in Canada as secretary to Sir Edmund Head, the successor of Lord Elgin, in the spirit of his own axiom that a man who means to climb a ladder does not establish himself on the lowest step. I am told that he also declined a small governorship in the West Indies, probably, if this is true, for the same reason; but to remain inactive, waiting upon fortune, was impossible to him. The plan which he had reluctantly resigned in order to accompany Lord Elgin now came back to his mind with double force; and he soon found an opportunity to explain and press his views. " I proposed," he says, "to Lord Clarendon that I should undertake a mission to Schamyl, for the purpose, if possible, of concocting some scheme with that chieftain by which combined operations could be carried on, either with the Turkish contingent, which was then just organised by General Vivian, or with the regular Turkish army." He never ceased to believe that great things could have been done had this plan been carried out,—that the fall of Kars might have been averted, and most sensible assistance given in the carrying out of all the objects of the war. He had scarcely got back to London, plunging again into all the excitement of that momentous time when the Crimea and the struggle going on there was the universal topic, than he flashed forth a pamphlet on this subject, calling the general attention to his project. Perhaps Lord Clarendon, then no doubt harassed with many suggestions, considered it the easiest way at last of getting rid of the eager young man, whose arguments were unanswerable and his perseverance boundless, to send him off to the heart of the diplomatic strife at Constantinople, and thus transfer the trouble of settling the question to other shoulders than his own. " He determined to send me with a letter to Lord Stratford de Redcliffe, authorising him to send me to Daghestan, in the Eastern Caucasus, where Schamyl had his stronghold, for the purpose of making certain overtures to him, at his lordship's own discretion."

It is difficult not to believe that Lord Clarendon's sanction to the journey which Laurence
was so eager to undertake was more in the nature
of a permission, accompanied by an introduction
to Lord Stratford, than anything more authoritative. The young man, however, took it in
a weightier sense, and set out in the highest
spirits, accompanied by his father, whose delight
in escaping from the uncongenial crowd of London, and in the prospect of exciting scenes and
experiences, seems to have been even greater
than that of his son. A compunction momen-
tarily clouded the mind of Laurence at the
thought of the mother left alone behind, with
the chief objects of her existence both gone : but
he comforted himself with the thought of the
visits to kind friends which she was about to
pay in the meantime, and the ministrations of
a kind and dear Lucy, a favourite niece, who
would console her ; and also with an immediate
effort to keep her amused by the most lively
account of the journey, and everything that he
and " Papa " said and did. Papa appears in an
altogether delightful light in this history. Of
course he picks up the greatest snobs on board
to be kind to, as Lady Oliphant will understand
—he keeps his end of the table full of jokes and
mirth, he enjoys everything with the freshness

of a boy, and with still more delighful freedom
and pleasure in novelty than even his son experiences.　　Laurence, indeed, becomes for the
time middle-aged and serious in presence of his
father's *insouciance* and charming boyishness.
The pair take the steamer at Marseilles for
Constantinople, and find themselves at once
drifted into the war atmosphere.　With them
in the ship is "Captain Speke of the Turkish
Contingent, formerly East India Company's service, who was speared in nine places on the coast
of Africa, where Burton, with whom he was, was
also wounded and their other companions killed.
Of course he is dying to go back and try again,
but is going to take a turn to Sebastopol first."
This is all that Laurence says of the great
traveller.　It is curious thus to meet undistin-
guished, before the events that made him famous,
passing across our vision for a moment, so well-
known a figure.　Another of more heroic mould,
Gordon, Laurence encountered in the trenches
before Sebastopol, but unfortunately there is no
record of that meeting.

　　Lord Stratford was not found at Constantinople,
and the travellers accordingly followed him in the
blazing August weather, up the Bosphorus to
Therapia.　The little steamer, which now fusses
so noisily yet so peacefully from village to village

along the shores of that glorious strait, breathed
nothing but gunpowder in those exciting days.
"The occupants of the boat were all Crimean
officers; none we actually knew, but we found
plenty of mutual acquaintance. It was exactly
like dining at a mess. Old friends met and
talked over their wounds and their dangers—some
boys of seventeen who have gone through the
whole thing, and were only anxious to get back.
One man would come and say, 'How are you, old
fellow?' and the old fellow, not remembering him,
would add, 'Were you not in the night attack?'
and then they would talk over old scenes, not
having seen each other since parted by cannon-
balls on that eventful night." At the house of
the English ambassador at Therapia, Laurence
was received with great kindness by Lord
Stratford, who talked to him much about the
war, taking the eager young diplomatist into his
confidence, and no doubt glad to hear from a new
witness so brilliantly observant and free from
officialism what was said and thought at home,
where already he had been misrepresented. The
ambassador ended by inviting his visitor to go
with him to the seat of war, whither he was just
about to start in his yacht in order to bestow
sundry decorations. Amid all his kindness and
confidential talk, he would not, however, say

anything about the mission to Schamyl, which
Lord Clarendon had left " to his lordship's discretion." Disappointed by this, yet pleased and
flattered by the place thus offered to him among
Lord Stratford's immediate surroundings, Laurence
resolved to accept his offer. "On the way," he
says, "I shall have plenty of time for imbuing
Lord S. with my own notions, and if he does
not succumb to my diplomacy in the end, I shall
consider myself too stupid to cope with Schamyl,
and be consoled."

"As I look out of my bedroom window," he
adds, "I see nothing but confusion; the whole
quay covered with French troops grouped round
their knapsacks, and going off in boats to the
steamers, while bullock-waggons containing heavy
baggage wheel along the water's edge, and busy
steamers of all sizes are passing up and down the
Bosphorus in such numbers that people never look
at them." The traveller of the present day, who
has felt how much the lovely peacefulness of those
beautiful shores is enhanced by the stream of
vessels of all descriptions that go up and down
from the Black Sea to the more peaceful waters
of Marmora and the busy port of the Golden
Horn, will be able to form some small idea of the
commotion and excitement of that moment, when
the white sails and peaceful fleets of trade were

swept out of the straits, and the transports and ships of war, bound to and fro to replenish the ranks with fresh troops and bring back the wounded and fever-stricken, were all that were visible. Yet even in the midst of this absorbing commotion, the young self-sent envoy, palpitating with eager projects, had time for affectionate and serious thought.

"I need not say that you are never absent from my thoughts, in the midst of all my plans more than ever; feeling how deeply you are interested in every one of them, and above all feeling how anxious you must be. I find myself, therefore, referring to you mentally at every moment, and the only thing that gives me anxiety is the fear that you may be so worried and anxious as to interfere with your health. Just in proportion as my present life is one to cause you anxiety do I constantly recur to you. When I was gay and thoughtless in Canada, I did not think half so much about you as now when I have got more weighty matters in hand. I hope you quite see the propriety of not missing such an opportunity of conferring with Lord S. as my voyage with him to the Crimea offers. I have been lying on my back for an hour reading and praying. I think it has done me good and strengthened my faith.

I feel ready for anything that God may see fit,—
for disappointment, I hope, as well as success."

It is impossible not to feel that now and then
his mother's call upon him for spiritual confidences,
and a report of all his thoughts, gave the young
man a certain impatience, and that he satisfied
her desire for information as to the state of his
soul, sometimes with utterances which must have
startled her, sometimes with attempts, not very
successful, to fall into the more ordinary vein of
religious musings. And there is always apparent
a little relief in getting back to the things of this
world, which it was more easy to treat. " I hope
to get Sir E. Lyons and General Simpson to see
the propriety of a Circassian expedition," he says,
carried away from his halting religious revelations
to the more eager tide of his hopes, " and if so,
shall insist upon being accompanied by a strong
military force, which will give a weight to my
representations which would be wanting to a
solitary agent." It is evident from the uncertainty and anxiety of these utterances that Lord
Clarendon's recommendation to Lord Stratford
must have been more a favourable one of a
remarkable and highly gifted young man, than
anything in the shape of official instructions to
the ambassador.

His next letter is dated from Kamiesch Bay, and gives a curious sensation of the very atmosphere and breath of war. "Long before we saw land we saw the vivid flashes of the guns, and heard the reports when we got nearer: a heavy cannonade was kept up all night. Very curious," he adds, "to be rigging out in ball costume (to dine in the Royal Albert, the Admiral's ship) to the sound of the booming guns of the bombardment. After dinner we watched the bombardment from the stern of the vessel,— sometimes the flashes rapid and close together, and the noise of the cannonading very great; at others it died away for a time." With their glasses they could see the shells whizzing through the air, falling in the trenches, and the rush of the soldiers in all directions. Few spectacles could be so exciting. In the meantime Laurence had given the ambassador his pamphlet to read, with the opinions of which Lord Stratford expressed his full agreement. "He has done everything but promise to send me to Schamyl," the young man adds; "that he staves off, and says he will think about it, &c. Though he can show no good objections, still he does not take to the scheme kindly." Laurence was not yet experienced enough to understand how different a thing it was to silence a statesman in argument, so that he could "show no good objections," and to get him to take in hand a visionary though hopeful scheme.

Arrived at the camp, Laurence describes to his mother the innumerable lines of tents, some miserable indeed, some comfortable enough, in which he finds as best he can a friend here and there, and snatches an exciting taste of this life of the camp, in which every pulse of existence was at the highest pressure, all the more stormy and strong in their beating from the constant disaster about, and the frequent carrying past of strings of dying and wounded men. The perpetual sound of the guns soon becomes familiar. "Since I have been here there has not elapsed a single minute, either by day or night, in which I have not heard the report of cannon." One of his objects while he roams among the lines is to find a tent for "Papa," from whom he has been obliged to separate in consequence of his invitation to accompany the ambassador, but who followed him to the camp, and remained a most interested and excited spectator of the extraordinary life there, after Laurence himself had hurried on to further and more wonderful experiences still.

On board the Royal Albert, on the occasion of the dinner-party which took place, while sky and water thrilled with the extraordinary sensation of shot and shell, Laurence had met the Duke of Newcastle, who had planned some sort of visit to the Circassian coasts, and who immediately invited the young man to join him. It is curious to note how, as soon as he appears on the scene, this irresistible young man connects himself with all that is highest and most influential near him. He seems to have kept the Duke's proposal in reserve as a sort of *pis aller*, not without a practical consciousness that an invitation from an ex-Minister and influential political personage was not one to be neglected, yet more intent upon his own plan than on any kind of social promotion. At last, scarcely because convinced by Laurence's reasoning, yet perhaps yielding a little to the influence of his strong conviction, Lord Stratford sent Mr Alison, one of his own staff, on a special mission to Circassia in H.M.S. Cyclops, with instructions to confer with Mr Longworth—the agent in charge of British interests along the coast-line, where many forts and villages had been taken from the Russians—upon the possibilities and advantages of a diversion such as was proposed; and, as Laurence believed, to consult as to the practicability of his own anxiously desired mission to Schamyl. As this latter, however, never came to anything, it may be permitted to the reader to believe that the ambassador was glad to occupy the eager young applicant by packing him off in attendance upon this envoy, and thus keeping him amused at a distance while grave questions were being discussed.

Laurence set out with high hopes, thinking that at last his somewhat quixotic and adventurous purpose was in a fair way of being carried out. And for the next three months he was kept cruising about the coast, now feeling his object almost within his reach, now further off from it than ever. He was in the midst of a little group of officials who were by no means sorry to have the help of his ready wit, and who enjoyed his cheerful company, but there is no appearance that his plan was ever taken into serious consideration at all. As time went on, and doubts on this subject began to cross his mind, he took great pains to justify himself to his mother for going on with an adventure which was evidently very pleasing in itself, though it did not carry out his intentions. " Besides writing to you," he says, " I have got the 'Times' to write long letters to. I look upon this as a great duty, because it brings me in lots of tin, and it is the only way I can justify my present life. I feel that in no other way could I be making so much

money by my own efforts." This most excellent
reason for continuing in a position so agreeable to
him Laurence puts forth, however, with so many
repetitions, that we feel he is not himself quite
satisfied with it, perceiving no doubt that, notwithstanding the "lots of tin," and the still more consolatory sense that he was the only Englishman
who could give the British public any real information on the subject which he felt to be so
important a one, he was not at all carrying out
the great plan of public benefit and private ambition with which he had started.

Amid all the adventures and excitements of
this strange life, however, he always found time
to gratify his mother by that report of his more
serious thoughts, and the progress of his spiritual
life, for which she was always asking.

" I am constantly thinking about these things,"
he says. " I am afraid, however, I generalise
too much, and am rather getting into a way of
overlooking ceremonies. I cannot but think that
if a man tries to act honestly and uprightly and
singly, the details of the thing are of comparatively little importance ; but then I also find that
you need the details as helps. It is a great
mistake to attach the importance we do to the
inherent virtue of these details, and misleads us.

Let every man find out which details help him
most, and adhere to them. Looked on in this
light, I think Sunday is a valuable detail. I look
upon your letters as a detail to help me : the day
I get them is much more of a Sunday to me than
any other.

"I feel strongly the love of God for me, and
thankfulness to Him, and great fear of offending
Him. I only do not always think that I am
offending Him, when you and others would think
that I did. The more I think of Him, the more
glorious does His service appear, and I dread that
I might fall into sin, and am sorry that I do not
keep a strict watch on my conversation, and I
do not think He hides Himself from me when I
pray."

"When one is knocking about and seeing so
much," he adds in another letter, "one does not
always, when the mail is going out, feel able to
write seriously or thoughtfully. Besides, when I
am happy, I am sorry to say I am more contented
with myself, and I often think it is difficult to
know how much of one's anxiety about the future
depends upon one's troubles in the present : when
these are removed, one is apt to think less of
one's soul. Innocent amusement is the most
deadening of anything. Frantic gaiety brings
its stings of conscience, but calm enjoyment

produces a permanent *kief* which should be watched."

It is seldom that so keen a piece of self-observation as the above comes from the pen of a young man enjoying to the full, as he was doing, all the delights of a life of adventure. He adds, on another occasion, some remarks on the subject of the conversion of a friend to Roman Catholic belief, which throws a light of another kind on after-incidents of his own life. " It is because he has not a strong will of his own that he wants to be dictated to on points of faith. Whately says it is the greatest exercise of man's private judgment to submit it to another. It is only the exercise of a weak judgment." These are very strange words to come from one who in after-years put this abnegation of judgment to so strong a proof. He describes himself as always having had " a mania for finding out what people believe," and holding theological discussions with many of the people with whom he is thrown into contact to this end. " He has a creed of his own," he says of one friend ; " but, like most people, has never really and philosophically considered the Bible." In another he comments on the " calm Episcopalianism " of a man who contents himself with externals, and does not trouble himself with thinking,—a state of mind for which the lively spectator finds a great deal to be said.

Thus he occupied the time of inaction, cruising in the Cyclops, running errands from one port to another, complaining occasionally of want of occupation, yet in constant activity, picking up every scrap of information that came in his way, and resolving to learn Circassian, to perfect his studies in Turkish, and generally to qualify himself as the only Englishman thoroughly acquainted with the subject. At this time he was still certain that Circassia was the key of the position, and that the current of the war would necessarily flow thither as the best way of effectually crippling and checking Russian advance. So far as he himself was concerned, his idea was that, if he knew the language, and " got up the country thoroughly," Government would not be able to do without him, " either here or in Parliament "; while he always continued to hold the conviction that, but for the premature conclusion of the war, Circassia would certainly have been the next point of operations, and the most effectual.

It gave a little renewed impetus to his thoughts and plans when, first, Omar Pasha, at the head of a Turkish force, supplemented by English artillery, appeared on the scene ; and secondly,

the Duke of Newcastle, still bent upon some brief
expedition upon Circassian territory. There were
many consultations between the Turkish general
and the English officials, in which Laurence took
a part, pleased, as he says, " to have to give my
opinion as an independent swell"; and for a time
it seemed possible that Omar might take the
matter into his own hands, and that the mission
to Schamyl, or if not to Schamyl, at least to
Schamyl's brother-in-law, the Naib of the Western
Caucasus, might still come into effect. But Omar
changed his mind at the last moment, when the
eager young would-be envoy was actually in the
saddle, and the only real result of his schemes
was a hunting expedition of a few days with the
Duke of Newcastle's party, into the country
which Laurence had so hoped to revolutionise.
In his account of this he says : " The Circassians
are delighted to receive us; but it is not easy
to make a duke go ahead enough to please me."
And indeed there is something almost ludicrous
in the idea of the grave middle-aged statesman,
weary with the cares of office and the troubles
of life, pricked on by this fiery boy in the full
tide of his own young unreasoning ambition and
impulses, always endeavouring to push his leader
forward, and convert the hunting-party into a
political mission.

"Of course, as every step is on ground never before traversed by Europeans, every step was interesting; and the scenery was beautiful, but the roads dreadful,—up almost perpendicular mountains and along the brink of precipices. The weather was heavenly all the time, and I would have given the world to go over the snow mountains, instead of contenting ourselves with getting to the base of them." The party had, however, a *grande chasse* at Prince Michael's, in which they did not kill much, but found it "very good fun." "I live a most vagrant life," he adds; "I just sleep where I happen to be when night comes on, —one night on board the Highflyer (the Duke's ship), the next on board the Cyclops, the next in Prince Michael's palace or shooting-box, the next in a hut." I have been told that during this period, when the eager young man was straining at his leash, eager for fun and occupation, he proposed to the captain of the Cyclops to make a sudden raid into a certain nook in shelter of an island, where he had discovered that a Russian man-of-war had put in secretly for repairs,—replying to the sailor's remonstrance that he would be disobeying his orders by doing so with a "What would that matter? Everything is pardoned to success."

However, dukes and schemes of all kinds passed

away, and there remained only Omar Pasha with his army, still holding out the hope of that campaign which Laurence had always looked forward to as the most effectual step that could be taken. He set out with the vanguard in great excitement and delight, slightly tempered by compunctions as to his mother's alarms, and fears lest this should be thought something very different from the hopes with which he started; yet much consoled by the letters to the 'Times,' which brought in "lots of tin," and kept the country supplied with information which no other Englishman could give. The Turks proved themselves excellent soldiers, and the scattered Russian forces left in Circassia fell back before them, only attempting an engagement on the banks of the Ingour river, in which Laurence was more actively engaged than he liked at first to confess. His first account to his mother gives the impression of great caution on his part. He "did not expose himself at all"—taking refuge in a hut, upon the roof of which, it is true, the bullets fell like rain, but where he professes to have been quite safe. The only moment of risk was "when I got your letter of 11th October, which was given me on the field by an officer just arrived from Constantinople, and in which you wonder when and where I would receive it.

There was a pretty brisk shower of missiles flying about, and I lay down under a bank and read it. On one side our great guns were blazing away, on the other the wounded were being carried past. Altogether it was about as odd a place to receive a letter in as you could have chosen. However, be thankful that I never was better in my life, barring that I have had nothing to eat for thirty-six hours except your letter (which I devoured) and a biscuit."

In another letter he is led on to mention " my battery," and this elicits the following anecdote :—

" By the by, I never told you I had made a battery. Skender Pasha, the officer in command, thought I was an officer from my having a regimental Turkish fez cap on, and asked me if I knew where a battery was to be made about which he had orders. It so happened that I did, because I had been walking over the ground with Simmons in the morning; so Skender told off a working party of two hundred men, with two companies of infantry and two field-pieces, put them under my command, and sent me off to make the battery. It was about the middle of a pitch-dark night, slap under the Russian guns, about two hundred yards from them. Luckily they never found us out, we worked so quietly. I had to do everything,—line the wood with sharp-shooters, put the field-pieces in position, and place the gabions. Everybody came to me for orders in the humblest way. In about three hours I had run up no end of a battery, without having a shot fired at me, while Simmons,[1] who was throwing up a battery a few hundred yards lower down, had a man killed. Both these batteries did good service two days after. The difficulty was, none of the officers with me could speak anything but Turkish. Afterwards Skender Pasha was speaking to Simmons about it, complaining of the want of interpreters, and instancing the English officer who made the battery not having an interpreter; so Simmons said, 'Ce n'est pas un officier, ce n'est qu'un simple gentleman qui voyage,' which rather astonished old Skender. I think Simmons looks on the 'Times' correspondent with a more favourable eye since that experience.

"I assure you it is quite an act of self-denial on my part leaving the army. I have no doubt I could get a command if I stayed; but don't be in the least alarmed. I have not the remotest intention of turning soldier, and only did that for fun and because of the consequences; besides, I knew if we worked quietly they would never find us out. They were rather astonished

[1] Now General Sir J. Lintorn Simmons, G.C.M.G.

at daybreak to see a battery mounting a couple
of guns staring them in the face, and began to
pound away at it with their rifles; but it was
too late, and they got as good as they gave.
Simmons had described to me in the morning
exactly where the battery was to be made, and
how to make it. So the whole thing turned out
very fortunately."

In case the mother at home should think that
those fortunate and fortuitous accidents which
made it happen that Laurence should know all
about the battery, and be thus able to act upon
an emergency, implied any inclination to risk
himself, he hastens to reassure her on this point.
" I hope you give me credit for prudence now,"
he says, " and will trust me. I assure you I was
in a horrible fright of getting shot, entirely on
your account, and I don't recommend a man to
come to fight if he has got anybody at home who
loves him. I don't think he can do his duty. If
it had not been for you, I should have taken an
active part in the affair. Altogether, though it
was in some respects a horrible experience, I am
glad to have seen it." This was the only real
passage of arms in the whole campaign, and a
long pause ensued at Sugdidi, where Laurence's
reports turn again to less exciting matters, and

to his own thoughts. The external life of the camp is thus graphically described :—

" I am very jolly here in Sugdidi—such a pretty place—only we can't plunder. It is a great temptation. I don't wonder at soldiers going to all lengths. One does not feel it is a bit wrong. I put a fine cock in my pocket this morning. I would have given his owner anything he asked if I could have found him ; but if we don't forage we get nothing but rice and biscuits to live on. I should not plunder anything but food, and that I don't call anything. I am not sure," he adds, "that I am not happier, occupied as my mind is now. It is when I have time to think much that doubts arise. When I just say my prayers and read a text earnestly, and then go and gallop about and am in hard healthful exercise, I feel much better in mind and body. I feel my mind much more innocent and less bothered and perplexed ; but I am afraid this is wrong, and that one's occupations ought to be God's work, and not what papa calls playing one's self."

I may be permitted to add one more of the common-sense and reasonable views of religious life, in opposition at once to the conventionality of many of the so-called evangelical tenets, and of much of his own after-thoughts, which are to be found scattered through these letters. "I wish," he says (a desire in which I am unable to follow him), "that the whole Bible was like David's compositions, and that such texts as 'If I pleased men I should not be the servant of Christ,' were not in it."

"It appears to me that to be a faithful servant of God, it is not necessary that one should be displeasing to His creatures; and that, constituted as they are, he pleases them most who, by an upright, straightforward conduct, pleases God most. The world does not like wicked men, and those points in which Christians displease the world are those which are involved in the peculiarities of the system, so to speak, which do not really affect a man's moral conduct. . . . There is not a single thing which my reason tells me I ought to do, which if I did people would find fault with. I am not in the least ashamed to say, even in the most dissipated society, that I believe immorality, which is regarded as the most venial of all sins, is wrong; but I am ashamed to say that I think going out shooting on Sunday is wrong, simply because I cannot understand why it should be, though I admit that it may be a valuable exercise of self-denial occasionally, and

that Sunday may be what I said the other day
—a very useful detail. I am afraid you will
think from this that I am in an unsatisfactory
state of mind; and so I am—chiefly, I think,
because I do not feel satisfied with holding views
different from many who I think are spiritually
enlightened. These, at least, are my camp
thoughts, and you asked me always to write
what I was thinking. But you may imagine
mine is not a life now to foster thought; and
if I had never led any other, I daresay I should
have been as good an Episcopalian as Ballard,[1]
and perhaps he is on that account the happier
of the two."

I think very few writers on religious subjects
have recognised the fact that many utterances
in the Bible of this description relate to a totally
different state of affairs from any existing among
ourselves, and that a man who makes it apparent
that he serves God truly is in no sense an unpopular man on that account. Indeed in most cases
it is quite the reverse, and goodness is the best
passport to universal respect. It pays, as Laurence
would have said—which is perhaps less acceptable

[1] Colonel John Archibald Ballard, C.B., commanding the artillery
attached to Omar Pasha's army, with whom much of Oliphant's time
was spent during this period, and for whom he had a high regard.

to many minds than the idea that it naturally involves persecution.

Here is another scrap which no doubt made the heart of the mother thrill with grateful pleasure, yet the overpowering sense of danger escaped. He has been describing the shooting of a spy.

"A single execution like this has far more effect upon me than when I see the ground strewn with dead bodies. One then somehow forgets they are men; and when we had a little quiet rifle-shooting on the banks of the Ingour before the battle, I looked at the men opposite as if they had been deer, and adjusted our fellows' sights for them, and watched the effect of the shots without the slightest feeling of compunction. Once, when I was sketching the river, and a fellow took a pot-shot at me, I took a rifle to return it from a man near; but then I remembered my promise to you, and his humanity, and crept away. The fellows Omar sent to sketch the river funked it; so I did a good deal in that line — crawling about on my hands and knees among the bushes, and flattering myself I was not seen. Whenever I was informed of this fact by the whizz of a Minié, I mizzled off to a safer place. I tell you all this instead of at the time, because the fighting is over; and so you have no cause to fear a recurrence of this amusement.   But it was very exciting, with the satisfaction, at the same time, of being really of use.   It was really sketching under difficulties."

Then the pendulum of thought swings back again to those subjects of which his home letters are always full.   He accuses himself over again of being moved by his present conditions at the moment, to piety or the reverse.   When he is in trouble, he is seized with "a sulky fit of devotion."   "Because, remember," he continues, "my religion at those times is not of a happy character; but I am gloomy and disgusted when I am trying to go to religion for comfort.   Somehow or other something ought to come of it all, for I am always thinking of the subject in some shape or other.   My conscience is never satisfied with my conduct, nor my understanding with my belief, so that altogether I live in a state of internal conflict and argumentation; and I would desire nothing more earnestly than to be a devoted Christian.   I admit that it involves giving up much that I now cling to; but I think I would not regret giving them up.   The best prescription I can think of is to live a month with Ernest Noel; intercourse with him seemed to do me more good than anything else."   It is seldom that the conflicting thoughts of a young man are thus clearly, and with so little conventional restraint, laid before another.

The campaign was brought to an end in the first place by the retreat of the Russians, afterwards by the disastrous news of the fall of Kars, which there had still been a hope of recovering; and finally, which was in the eyes of Laurence almost as great a disaster, by the sudden and unsatisfactory peace. And at last he is able to comfort his mother with news of his approaching home-coming, and of his projects for work and patience, and the conviction that an established position of one kind or another must await him. " I do not think that, though my prospects are no more definite than they were, I shall be so miserable and unsettled. I feel more of a philosopher. I have satisfied myself about this question, and intend to be independent. I can write what I know and other people don't. If there is a general election, I shall certainly try hard to get in, but I hate the idea of asking anybody for anything now. I think I can get on in spite of them."

It was the very end of the year before Laurence got home from this brilliant, exciting, and entirely ineffectual journey. He had made many new acquaintances, both in places and people, and heard a great deal which he expected to be superlatively useful to him, but which, except in so far as it supplied material for a book, was of scarcely any utility at all. But he was no nearer a definite mode of establishing himself in life than he had been when he set out. He returned after an illness — caught in the wet and cold of the tents and the hardships of the march, which was in reality a retreat, "not before the enemy but the weather," and attended by many depressing and wretched details,—in the last days of 1855 or beginning of 1856. He came home in the vein I have quoted, determined to make his own way and ask nothing from anybody, and with his mind divided between the diplomatic service and Parliament—a career towards which he had already directed his thoughts. I think it was during this period that he first contested the Stirling burghs, though without success; but of this incident I find no details.

This waiting, however, for something to turn up, Micawber-like, as he himself describes it, was so little to his mind, that in the following summer he was again on the war-path, seeking employment, adventure, or whatever might befall him. Unfortunately (though perhaps it is as well for the space at my disposal), I have not succeeded in obtaining any of the letters of this period, so that it can only be traced through those recollections which he thought fit during his life to give to the public. From these it would appear that, notwithstanding all his philosophical resolutions, his impatience of his own want of progress soon reached a great height, and that he was ready for anything that involved movement and activity, finding himself no doubt at the same time more or less independent, so long as he had something novel and strange to tell, by reason of that connection with the 'Times,' which made the wildest wandering profitable. Accordingly, he left England again in the course of the summer of 1856, at first in company with the well-known Mr Delane of the 'Times,' to whom " I was able," he says, " to act as cicerone on our arrival at New York," and whose enjoyment of the society and ever - abounding hospitality of that capital was no doubt much enhanced by the popularity and universal acquaintanceship of his young companion, whose previous experiences as Lord Elgin's brilliant secretary were still recent. What the business was in which the young man was engaged, I am not aware; but he speaks of it in a letter to Mr Leveson-Gower as likely to put a thousand pounds in his pocket. When this was accomplished, Laurence went on

upon his adventurous way, and, with a keen
scent for excitement to come, turned his steps
to the Southern States, with the idea, first,
of making himself acquainted on the spot with
the workings of slavery, as well as with the
peculiar social conditions of that section of the
American world. "From what I saw and
heard," he says, "it was not difficult to predict the cataclysm which took place four years
later, though the idea of the South resorting to
violence was scouted in the North; and when,
upon more than one occasion, I ventured to sug-
gest the possibility to Republicans, I was invariably met by the reply that I had not been long
enough in the country to understand the temper
of the people, and attached an importance it did
not deserve to Southern 'bounce.'" His visit to
that old-new world of the plantations—the patri-
archal households and primitive innocent communities, bound by a hundred ties to their head,
which every picture, even of the most eager
Abolitionist character, permits us to see in the
slave-holding States, though neutralised by the
horrible possibility of a traffic in human flesh and
blood—was full of interest to him.

Laurence found his way as usual among "the
best people," and his stay at New Orleans was
"one of unqualified enjoyment." But it is a

practical evidence of his extreme impatience with
the as yet undetermined lines of his own life,
that he should have been attracted by the idea
of an expedition to which the nickname "filibuster," one of the most felicitous coinages of
Americanism, was applied—a word of nonsense,
aptly expressing with humorous scorn, yet impartiality, the sound and fury, the big intention
and pretence, of the modern pirate, half-swagger,
half-serious meaning. That Laurence Oliphant,
who was still well within the reach of good
fortune at twenty-seven, and who was soon to
fill a responsible and important place in actual
diplomatic service, should have " accepted a free
passage to Nicaragua in a ship conveying a rein-
forcement to Walker's army," and should have
carried " strong personal recommendations to that
noted filibuster," is one of the most curious
events in his career. This strange step was
taken chiefly, no doubt, " for fun," as when he
made his battery,—but also a little, we can scarcely doubt, from feelings much more serious, and
originating in one of those fits of partial despair
and disgust with his surroundings, and the lack
of advancement, which has been the cause of so
many wild enterprises. Walker was requested
by his agent, Mr Soulé, in New Orleans, " to
explain the political situation to me, in the hope

that, on my return to England, I might induce
the British Government to regard his operations
with a more favourable eye than they had hitherto done. The fact that if I succeeded I was to
be allowed to take my pick out of a list of con-
fiscated *haciendas*, or estates, certainly did not
influence my decision to go, though it may
possibly have acted as a gentle stimulant; but
I remember at the time having some doubts on
the subject, from a moral point of view. I remember spending Christmas Day in high spirits
at the novelty of this adventure upon which I
was entering." The Christmas before he had
been at Trebizond, just emerging from the hardships of Omar Pasha's campaign. But during
all the vicissitudes of his Circassian adventures,
he had more or less the prestige of a member of
the British diplomatic service. Now, however,
in strange contrast to that reflected dignity,
he was setting forth on what was distinctly a
piratical undertaking, amid a crew of armed ad-
venturers, invaders, bent on conquest. It was a
singular change, and one which we can scarcely
suppose could sit easily upon his mind in moments
of seriousness; but the fun and novelty, with perhaps something of the underlying impatience and
disgust of the ordinary which had driven him
from London, carried the day.

This adventure, however, was doomed to be but short; and much in the way in which a naughty prince, in a romance, would be arrested and conveyed back to his proper sphere, Laurence was shaken loose from his companions and carried off to his natural surroundings. When the filibuster ship came to the mouth of the San Juan river, its progress was impeded by "a British squadron lying at anchor to keep the peace," from one of the vessels of which a boat was soon pulling towards them. "A moment later Captain Cockburn, of H.M.S. Cossack, was in the captain's cabin making most indiscreet inquiries as to the kind of emigrants we were. It did not require long to satisfy him; and as I incautiously hazarded a remark which betrayed my nationality, I was incontinently ordered into his boat as a British subject, being where a British subject had no right to be. As he further announced that he was about to move his ship in such a position as would enable him, should fighting occur in the course of the night, to fire into both combatants with entire impartiality, I the less regretted this abrupt parting from my late companions, the more especially as, on asking him who commanded the squadron, I found it was a distant cousin. This announcement on my part was received with some incredulity, and I was taken on board the Orion, an 80-gun ship carrying the flag of Admiral Erskine, to test its veracity, while Captain Cockburn made his report of the Texas and her passengers. As soon as the admiral recovered from his amazement at my appearance, he most kindly made me his guest, and I spent a very agreeable time for some days, watching the emigrants disconsolately pacing the deck."

Thus our young man " fell on his feet" wherever he went, and instead of suffering at all for his wild and unjustifiable undertaking, found himself in excellent and amusing quarters, restored to all the privileges of his rank,—the admiral's cousin at sea being as good for all purposes as a king's cousin ashore. The moral of which would seem to be that, when you have a habit of getting into risky positions, the best thing in the world is to belong to a good Scotch family of " kent folk," with relations in every department of her Majesty's service both at home and abroad.

He would seem, however, though the letters fail at this period, to have been in a state of no small depression about his prospects, and more than usually sick of the uncongenial position of waiting till something should turn up, and besieging his official friends with applications, which is the usual position of a young man seeking advancement—or at least was, before the public services were ruled by examinations as at present. That he should have made such an expedition at all is a proof at once of the extraordinary detachment and independence of mind which afterwards made his life so remarkable, and of great impatience and dissatisfaction with ordinary circumstances, as well as of the love of adventure, which was always a leading trait in his character. He was so far independent that he had the means of moving about at his pleasure without any absolute necessity to work for daily bread,—a fact which gives wings to impatience, and makes every sudden movement practicable. His hot impulses were, however, stayed by the excellent expedient of legitimate occupation a few months after his return from his filibustering ; and in the month of April 1857 he set out with his old friend and chief, Lord Elgin, on his mission to China, occupying the post of private secretary once more.

CHAPTER VI.

THE MISSION TO CHINA.

IT is unnecessary here to enter further into the history of the operations in China than is wanted to explain the part which Laurence took in them. He has himself left a history of the mission and all its performances, in a narrative published immediately after its termination. Its importance in modern history was much greater than was even anticipated, seeing that it was not only the beginning of legalised and comprehensible dealings with China, but in some degree the means of discovering, diplomatically, and adding to the variety of Nature, the heretofore half fabulous, yet in reality most intelligent, wide-awake, and progressive, empire of Japan. The position of Laurence was still unofficial. He was not a recognised servant of the Foreign Office or member of the diplomatic service. Probably it was part of the disadvantage of his irregular education,

and partly of those independent ways and opinions which had always been characteristic of him,
that he never seems to have made any attempt
to constitute himself a regular member of this
profession which would seem to have been so
completely congenial to him. But there was
still at that time an accidental character about
that service, and chances for the man who was
proved capable, which were probably much more
attractive to him than the routine of a public
functionary.

I have been told by one of the other members of the expedition, Sir Henry Loch, then
an *attaché* serving his apprenticeship in the
service in which he now occupies so distinguished
a position, that the first appearance of Oliphant
among the group of young men in attendance
upon the Minister was somewhat startling to
those gilded youths. He began to talk, as they
lounged about the deck with their cigars, of
matters spiritual and mystical, singularly different
from the themes that usually occupy such groups.
They asked each other what strange comrade
they had here when they talked over the new
addition to their party. It would seem to have
been the then quite new development of what,
for want of a better name, people call spiritualism, or more vulgarly, spirit-rapping, which was

the subject of the talk about the funnel in the
soft tropical night. I find, however, no trace of
this in the letters, which give a wonderfully clear
view of what Laurence was thinking, and of the
point in his religious history to which he had now
come—which, as the reader will see, occupied his
mind very much even amid all the excitements of
the expedition. He would seem, during the interval between this and his former secretaryship
in Canada, to have completely burst the strait
bonds of his mother's evangelical views, then
holding him but lightly—as it seems inevitable
that a lively young mind awakening to demand
a reason for everything should do : and had now
come to something like a tenable foundation for
his personal belief—which differed much from that
in which he had been trained, yet which he was
very anxious to prove to be a most real rule of
life. Thus the expedition, which was so brilliant
and important, and out of the records of which
he made a book so readable, interesting, and
amusing, is associated in his private history with
the rising of religious thoughts and convictions
which ripened in the monotony of the many intervals of waiting which came between the exciting episodes of his life. Nothing can be more
curious than to see—between the fighting and the
exploring, which he enjoys like a schoolboy, al-

ways somehow finding himself in the front, always gay, amusing, and amused—the student retired in his cabin, hearing nothing but the monotonous swish of the waves, and pondering the ways of God to man, and especially the mistaken, confusing, and derogatory interpretations given by all human systems of these wonderful ways. Sometimes his own views are very strikingly expressed; but it is not necessary that the reader should agree with him in order to be interested in this curious second side of the versatile, delightful, gay, and adventurous young man, who was ready for everything—the ball-room and the council-chamber and the smoking-room, while still most warmly attracted of all by the book of theology which awaited him all the time in his retirement.

His parents would seem to have been established in the neighbourhood of London—I imagine at Spring Grove, a house within reach of his uncle's house at Wimbledon—when he left England; and to his mother it was always like a rending asunder of soul and body to part with him. He sends her a note from the Indus, the steamer in which he had set out to join the mission at Alexandria, hoping that she is not letting herself be miserable. "There are numbers of partings going now," he writes, "and weeping

parents going on shore; so you are not alone."
At Alexandria, where the new overland route
and the railway across the desert had just been
put in operation, he does not enter into any
details about the place, which was already
familiar both to himself and his correspondent,
but makes an amusing note on the subject of the
train coming in from Cairo, "quite a sight."
"There was a harem carriage, and Arabs were
clinging like flies to all parts, crowding the roof,
and even perched upon the buffers. They jumped
off like frogs long before the train stopped. I
believe a good many are killed monthly; but
they are cheap here, and certainly take kindly to
steam locomotion." At Cairo "we go about in
grand style, Lord Elgin in a state carriage, with
four grey horses, and a whole posse of horsemen
and running footmen, who at night carry blazing torches, making the whole procession very
picturesque. We follow behind in two other of
the Pasha's carriages, accompanied by sundry
beys and swells." At Galle, where on their
arrival the well-known place brought many
recollections to the traveller's mind, they were
met by the news of the breaking out of the
mutiny in India, which, however, does not seem
to have at once disturbed either the secretary or
his chief, as after-records announce. The mis-

sion went on, with a faint fear that this new contingency might interfere with the public interest in China, but apparently no graver apprehensions : until further and worse news met them at Singapore, the next halting - place in their journey.

Lord Elgin has always received great credit for changing, on his own responsibility, the destination of the troops who met him there— the small expeditionary army, without the support of which his mission could do nothing— and sending them on to India instead, thus affording the most valuable aid at an important moment. The extreme embarrassment and difficulty brought upon himself by this step has, however, received little notice, magnanimity in such a matter being generally, like virtue, its own reward. Laurence takes, however, even this credit from his chief, by an intimation that the troops were ordered to China by Lord Canning, to the dismay of the plenipotentiary, thus deprived of his army. It is difficult to come to the exact truth even on such a public matter ; for I have been assured by another member of the mission, not only that Lord Elgin took the initiative, but that it was on the advice of himself, as knowing India, that his lordship did so ! There is, however, no doubt as

to the next step, which was that Lord Elgin,
finding his own position thus diminished, and
moved by the tremendous difficulty and danger
of the crisis, himself followed the troops to
Calcutta to give Lord Canning his support, and
that, still more effectual, of a naval brigade from
the Shannon and Pearl. That there was some
policy in this movement, as well as a chivalrous
postponement of the interests of his own mission,
was perhaps more apparent at the time to the
members of the mission, thus arrested, than it was
to the general public. Lord Elgin was consoled
by a patriotic address from the merchants of
Singapore, whose interests were much concerned
in the success of his expedition, yet who concurred
wisely and sympathetically in the delay. As
these excellent men were not of a literary turn,
they had recourse to Lord Elgin's young secretary, who had already made himself universally
popular in the community, to write their address
for them,—a circumstance which did not in the
least detract from its perfectly genuine character,
but which Laurence related with much amusement
to his mother at home.

Nothing more self-denying than the step thus
taken could have been. It involved not only the
absence of all the prestige surrounding a splendid
expedition, but the surrender of the fine ship and

comfortable quarters provided for the envoy and his staff, and much miserable uncertainty, delay, and humiliation. And though they were received at Calcutta on their arrival with the greatest enthusiasm, the secretary's letters do not convey the idea that the magnanimous visitor had any great recompense for his sacrifice. " He scarcely sees a soul, and leads a dreary life in that dreary pile," says the young man, who is for his own part somewhat astonished to see the calm of Calcutta, the usual show of beauty and fashion on the ordinary promenade, and the usual hospitalities going on—a thing, no doubt, inevitable, but always jarring upon the nerves of the spectator. He himself, however, as a spectator, shared this calm. There is no appearance in his letters of excitement, though he was surprised by the ordinary look of everything around him. In the same house in which he was lodged were two ladies lately escaped at the risk of their lives, and under remarkable circumstances, on the eve of a massacre; but who drove out with himself and a friend in their buggies for the evening drive as if nothing had happened—curious composure of human nature, which assimilates the most wonderful events, and takes tragedy itself into the common current of every day!

The Chinese mission, however, were outsiders,

and had nothing to do personally with the Indian crisis. And when they returned again to the scene of their own duties humbly in a P. & O. steamer—the Ava—without any of the pomp of the splendid man-of-war, to kick their heels in Hong-Kong and wait until a detachment of 1500 soldiers should be sent to them from England, to fill the place of the 5000 men, soldiers and sailors together, whom they had parted with to India, it is little wonder if they were discouraged. The excitement of a great sacrifice is apt to have a *contre-coup* of vexation and depression. "We have sunk into such insignificance, and are in such a fix without an army," Laurence wrote on his return to Hong-Kong, "nor are the speeches of Sir C. Wood and other members of the Government very encouraging. How they expect Lord Elgin to carry out the same policy without any army which he was instructed to do with one, is not very clear." He adds, with a little amusing malice, "I have one consolation, that you will be much more relieved thinking of me living cooped up in a ship in harbour for the next three months, where there are neither women nor Chinese, than if I were doing anything else." It is apparent throughout that Lady Oliphant largely shared what is supposed to be a general feeling with mothers, against the intrusion of love into the hearts of their sons. She upbraids him sometimes as being heartless, when some instance of inadvertent fascination on Laurence's part rouses her pity for the lady whom he has loved and ridden away. Indeed it would appear to have been the truth that our young *diplomat*, always addicted to making himself agreeable, was still more so where ladies were concerned; and, whether by means of polkas or theological discussions, was wont to work considerable havoc upon his way through the world. His mother is glad to hear that he is in a place where such intercourse is impracticable; but Laurence himself does not like it. It is to be said for him, however, that he always informs her of his amusements in this way, keeping her, no doubt, in a flutter of alarm which he was apt to enjoy.

Yet with all this, these letters, which are so confidential, so full of the comradeship and equality which is rare between parents and children (there was, as I have said, only some eighteen years' difference in their age), so free in discussion and remark — continue to be filled above everything else with his religious views and feelings: the revelation of what he has come to in the way of conviction after much struggling, and tortures of doubt—and his indignant disapproval of the hackneyed types of Christianity with which he is acquainted. His first letter on this subject is in answer to an expression of much dissatisfaction on her part as to his views.

"Hong-Kong, 4th July [1857].

"All that related to J. pained me much, but so did that which related to myself. I thought you understood that it was no obstinacy on my part which compels me, before adopting a faith, to judge of the merits of its claim by the light God has given me. It is no light thing attributing to the Deity a work containing much that appears derogatory to His dignity. Nor is there any means whatever of knowing whether it is His or not, except by an exercise of the means He has given us. I do not in the least set up my reason against His, but against my fellow-creatures', who tell me to accept a book as from Him upon no better evidence than I myself possess, the chief reason being that it is better than any other, which I am quite ready to admit; but I feel that I should be sinning seriously against Him were I not very jealously to guard against adopting any system which involved what I consider degrading to Him, without overwhelming evidence of its authenticity. Such evidence must of necessity be supernatural, as everything coming through mortal agency is, *prima facie*, from the very nature of things, imperfect. I do not like to dwell on a subject which I know is painful to you, and I am afraid you will never understand what I mean, or, after all I have said to you, you would never have used the old arguments about not exercising my reason on what I do not understand. I certainly do not understand God's dealings with man, nor am I so presumptuous as to suppose I ever shall; but if I did not exercise my reason, there would be nothing to prevent my accepting the Koran or any other system of theology my fellow-creatures might assure me was right, and deny me the privilege of judging for myself. You say you would be glad if I could give up my career for God's service. I would willingly go into a dungeon for the rest of my days if I was vouchsafed a supernatural revelation of a faith; but I should consider myself positively wicked if upon so momentous a subject I was content with any assumptions of my erring and imperfect fellow-creatures, when against the light of my own conscience.

"With regard to prayer, I have lately been asking for things, because I could not endure, as it were, merely stating my case, and I felt so strongly what you say about answers; but it has been, and is, with a strong feeling of doubt

and disquietude that I am dishonouring Him
by supposing I can influence Him in anything.
However, I have too strong a sense of His love
to think it can be displeasing to Him; and the
instinct seems so deeply implanted in one to do
so, though I think it is only the instinct of a
low spiritual creature, and when one gets further
advanced one will not need it. However, it is
no pleasure to me to be thus distracted with
doubts and difficulties, and therefore pray do
not think I am doing it from a spirit of pride
or 'opposition. I am really anxious to know and
do what is right, though the circumstances of my
present life are unfavourable; and, moreover, I
do not attach importance to the infraction of
what are really the conventionalities of the
Christian world. I may appear to be irreligious
because my religion does not consist in the same
course of action, and my standard is different. I
do not say that I act up to it, but I think if I
did I should shame the professing Christian. My
faith is not strong enough to bring me up to my
standard, but I hope it may be some day.

"I quite agree in what papa says about the
spiritualist's God. I felt it myself. It removed
Him too far off. But, on the other hand, what
papa calls God's invention of Christ does not remove the difficulty: it substitutes another being,

whose merit is that you are to think of Him as God. The moment you think of Him as God, He is as far away as ever, besides the dire confusion which such a mixture immediately raises in the mind. I never from my earliest day could get over that difficulty, and always found myself instinctively yearning for the fountainhead, and overleaping all intermediate beings. However, I am glad you wrote, because it stirs me up. I get too distracted sometimes by my mode of life, and do not think so much as I ought. In order to keep up the proper peace of mind, one ought to be constantly thinking, and not contented with a morning and evening ejaculation. I would sooner go to the stake than do violence to what I believe to be the yearnings and whisperings, weak and imperfect no doubt, of my divine nature."

He returns to the subject of prayer on another occasion, quoting a passage from Francis Newman to illustrate his position. "So," he adds, "because I pray I do not feel that I can influence God, but that in expressing my desires I am holding almost the only communion which is open to me, giving Him, as it were, all my confidence, as the most pleasing homage I can do Him, and the fullest recognition I can make of His love and beneficence, and the interest He has in my happiness and welfare." This is little more than a modern expression of the same sentiment which John Knox stated, in far stronger and more eloquent words, when he described prayer as "an earnest and familiar talking with God." Laurence, however, had not, I fear, notwithstanding his many qualities, that preference for the best and highest in literature, either sacred or profane, which we expect to find in a mind so well endowed. Theodore Parker is the fount from which he chiefly draws in these religious speculations, and he finds pleasure in Longfellow which Tennyson does not convey. It is not necessary to be a critic because a man is full of native · ability and force of mind. The juxtaposition of these two names in poetry, with a preference for the former unhesitatingly and strongly expressed, will make most readers smile: but it would be vain to claim for him a perfection which he did not possess. Perhaps his early association with America, in the first independent opening of his mind, may have had something to do with it; perhaps his imperfect education, which fed him upon "good" books, and shut up to him the highest sources of poetical imagination. Some one, I do not remember who, tells of the excitement and delight with which he discovered

Shakespeare, who had been unknown to him—coming back and back to tell his amused friends of some new wonder in the book which they had recommended to him in the dearth of other reading. It is well to know that he was capable of being thus stirred : he was not capable, it is evident, of judging the respective magnitudes of the lesser lights.

The subject of religion, however, is far the most important to him, and continually in his thoughts. His feelings on this subject are saddened by the consciousness that his correspondent will not enter into them, but rather blame him for his views on many matters of faith. ·" A transition state," he says, " such as I am in, is never a favourable one ; but I do hope that I am getting hold of something. I have learnt, however, to believe in nothing which I cannot see manifested in life. The influence of early life, and the constraints which one set of opinions imposed, are loosened. Though another set of opinions may involve precisely the same restraints, time is required to ripen their influence. Of course, a man cannot bring a faith to bear upon his life and conversation until he has got a very firm hold of it."

The one point upon which he is assured is that this is his only test. He sees all round him men who are very nice fellows, who would be horrified not to be called Christians, but in whom religion of any kind is as little apparent as if they believed nothing. " I am a thorough Christian," he says, " so far as my reverence for and belief in every moral principle Christ has propounded is concerned; but I am utterly opposed to the popular development of Christianity,—indeed I think it quite inconsistent with His teaching. I never felt so deep an interest in any subject, and am thankful for the leisure I have had to read and think of it." The same sentiment appears again and again. " Those who have seen war," he says, "can best appreciate the value of Christ's ' Blessed are the peacemakers.'

" If that was to be the aim of the diplomatist, his would be the noblest of professions. My natural man is intensely warlike, which is just as low a passion as avarice or any other. I went last Sunday to church to hear a parson, with a Crimean medal on his surplice, preach between a lot of 68-pounders on 'Fear not man that can kill the body, but fear Him who can cast both body and soul into hell,' and I wondered what sort of morality you could expect from men whose occupation was the destruction of their fellow-creatures, to the conscientious discharge of which they were to be urged by their fear of an avenging Deity, the Creator of them all. One would think even a sailor would discern the impossibility of elevating his moral nature by the application of two such principles as cruelty and fear."

It is not my part to point out the fallacy as well as the strong *parti pris* of these remarks : they are intended to show the working of the mind, which it is my business to delineate in its weakness as well as in its strength.

" The more I consider my own nature," he adds, " the more I see the tremendous power a creed ought to contain within itself to become a living principle. A flaw here or there does infinite mischief. In order to prevail over the tendency to evil, it must invade with overwhelming force a man's whole nature, obliging him by its purity, and the strength of its appeal to his convictions, to recognise its truth ; but if his moral instincts discover the slightest flaw, the whole fabric goes by the board, and he has hard work to make up the leeway, which the absence of the old faith and the struggle for the new involves. I can well understand any man giving up in despair the hope of finding a creed containing elements powerful enough to govern him absolutely. It is a long time before he gets over a sort of repugnance at the very idea of the old one, and recognises again all that is good and beautiful in it. I do think that God satisfies every man's craving in this respect in time, if he keeps on fighting and groping."

It is very seldom that we have the spectacle of a mind thus seething with dissatisfaction and eager desire after a better way, so curiously unphilosophical in his philosophy, and so penetrated in the midst of his revolt by sentiments of reverential and strongly realised faith. Here is a very interesting exposition of his standing ground and its disadvantages :—

" In looking upon my own state and experience, I find to the good that I have made certain advances towards a faith which no doubt influences my life perhaps not more than my life used to be influenced before ; but the difference is that formerly my life depended not upon the sincerity of my moral convictions, or even on my fear of offending God, but entirely on the fear of making you miserable. Had that check ceased to exist, I have no doubt I should have gone to the

bad. The old associations and habitual restraints
might have held me in for a short time, but very
short, and the end would have been utter reckless-
ness or defiance. Now that is all changed, and
although, as I say, my present life may not be
better than my past, still it is founded on a different basis, and, I trust, will go on improving,
irrespective of any mundane event. That, I say,
I find to the good. To the bad I have to lament
an entire looseness in my moral tone and conversation, for which I can perfectly account, but
which I find it most difficult to overcome. It
arises from the contempt I feel (but which is
wrong) for professors of a creed which has no
power over them, but all the dogmas which I
am blamed for not subscribing to. When men
who keep harems go to church regularly, and
blame me for not going with them, I am apt to
confound the faith with the individual, and swear
at the whole concern. And so, because I do not
confess to a good deal that seems to be hollow in
the practice of a popular theology, I am put down
as being without religion, and so lose any influence which, did I refrain from this, I might have,
besides giving a totally wrong impression of my
real convictions. But it is a mistake to confound religion with theology. It is the fashion to
regard the former as springing from the latter,

whereas if you have the former it makes little difference what you profess as the latter.

"But do not think I confound the Christian religion with the practice which its professors follow, in accordance with a theology they have deduced from it. The Bible is a very different thing from the popularly received traditionary interpretation of it which rests on human reason. I quite believe in its inspiration, but in a particular way. I had first thought of an illustration when I found an almost exactly similar one in Morell. He proves, by a very well-argued and elaborate process, that revelation and intuition are the same thing. I had long arrived at that, but did not know how, until he proved it. Theodore Parker has the same; but my notion is this, that supposing a man's whole moral nature was in perfect harmony, and his spiritual intelligence perfect, his mind would be like a perfectly calm lake upon which would be accordingly reflected the mind of God; but the moment the surface is disturbed the image becomes imperfect, the amount of the imperfection depending upon the amount of the disturbance. Now, according to my view, the minds of Christ and of His apostles were in that state of almost perfect spiritual repose. They reflected more accurately than was ever done before or since the mind of God:

that is, the apostles caught their repose from the mind of Christ—but you see in them the imperfections of a disturbed moral nature. Peter and Paul quarrel, and attach importance to things strangled and to circumcision—that is, the surface was ruffled by old prejudices, undue spiritual enthusiasm, strong passions, &c.—and so fail to give that perfect image of the mind of God. We may perceive these imperfections, though very far from having minds so spiritually enlightened as theirs, just as you can tell the faults of a picture without being an artist. I feel sure that as men's minds become more enlightened, and they begin to receive those revelations which the apostles did themselves, they will no longer accord their writings the infallibility which they do not claim (they only claim inspiration, which, as I say, they certainly had, and which I trust others may yet have). The goodness of the inspiration must depend upon the medium. The purest inspiration may be polluted. If the channel is a sewer, it does not matter how clear may be the spring; so in the Old Testament we find all sorts of people chosen as mediums; but of the value, for instance, of Solomon's inspiration we must judge for ourselves. It is in accordance with the divine plan always to make use of human means, with all their imperfections, and I see no reason to suppose that the Bible is the only thing that ever came through human instruments that does not partake of their imperfections, more especially when the internal evidence that it does so is irresistible to my mind."

He adds, that in the midst of the rising excitement of an approaching crisis, which in former times would have occupied him wholly, he feels himself much more interested in metaphysical questions than in the bombardment of Canton, or anything that can happen. His guides in these researches seem to have been Theodore Parker, to whom he constantly refers, and Mr Morell, whose 'History of Philosophy' had recently made an impression upon the public attention which has not proved permanent. It is unfortunate that a mind so active, yet which was never without a certain confusion in these matters—which, curiously enough, he proclaims at this period as his favourite study — should not have been under more thorough and trustworthy guidance. It seems a paradox, yet it is one of which there are many examples, that when a mind essentially practical, with a special literary gift of clear narrative, involves itself in metaphysical subjects, this strange confusion is often the result. General Gordon is another example of a heroically keen intelligence in practical effort and dealings with

men, which yet became hopelessly clouded and
bewildered in theological matters, wandering in
a fog of chaotic thought, and substituting subject
for object, and *vice versâ*, with a boldness which
is also heroic, though sadly perplexing to the
reader. Laurence Oliphant's religious theories at
this moment, when he pursued them hotly in his
cabin, amid all the curious surroundings of an
expedition which was at once diplomatic and
military, will show how ready his mind was for
the influences which afterwards took possession
of it,—how superficial in theory, how heroic in
determination to follow out his conclusions to
whatever end they might lead.

Meantime, as he says, the plot was thickening
around, and had it not been for this preoccupa-
tion with metaphysics and the religious question,
" I ought now to be in an intense state of excitement.

" Wade has gone up the river with a flag of
truce and Lord Elgin's ultimatum to Yeh. I
volunteered to go ; but he was quite right not
to send me, not being a Chinese scholar, though
I begged hard. The Admiral has drawn a cordon
close round Canton, and is to occupy the island
of Homan, immediately opposite the town, to-
morrow. The French fleet has gone up the river

to take part in the blockade. The 59th and artillery go up with the General; in a day or two we shall have upwards of 6000 men as a land force, half red jackets and half blue, including the French. If Yeh does not give in, they will take Canton on Tuesday week, the 22d, probably. I do not anticipate any great difficulty even if he holds out; but the bazaar report here is that he is in a horrid fright, and going to give in and come to terms. I hope he may, for in case of bombardment of a town containing a million of people, the slaughter of innocent women and children and people generally will be dreadful. However, the bishop has appointed a day of humiliation for the Indian business; so we are to humble ourselves to-day, and make up for it next week by sending a few thousands of our fellow-creatures into the next world."

On a similar subject he enlarges at more length in a following letter :—

" I see you have been having a great day of humiliation. I am very strongly opposed to this, as very derogatory to God and reflecting upon His love. He has created a universe with certain laws; all violation of these laws implies misery—a misery which is ordained to teach men to improve themselves. The child trying to walk tumbles and hurts its nose. It was no judgment on the child that it fell : it was a wise law that provided a misery, and its humiliation consisted in keeping its legs straight for the future. It is a mockery to say you are sorry, and go and do the same again ; and a sin to think that God acts by fits and starts as we do, with a judgment here and there, as if the whole thing was not obedient to fixed and certain laws. The general notion is that you are appeasing an angry Deity, which is the worst of all."

It is curious that this very *banal* though plausible view of national prayer, the frequent utterance of the superficial thinker, had been already met and answered by himself in the individual point of view a few letters before, as above quoted. After so many details of these opinions as to the demerits of Christians and merit of Christianity, and his own uncomfortable substitution of the one for the other, which is very much what they come to, the reader will be refreshed by his thoughts upon another subject —one, too, of the greatest importance to him in after-life, and of which it is apparent here he already held the germ. His mother's letter had informed him of the death of their friend Dr

Clark, which he says gave him at first a painful shock :—

" We have been so accustomed to surround death with horrors, and to be selfish in our sorrow, that news of the departure from the world of any one we love gives us quite a different feeling from what it ought. No doubt this partly arises from an uncertainty whether we shall ever meet again, and a want of faith in the love of God, who, I feel certain, will never separate people for long who love one another. In the meantime, I have no doubt Tom is often present with us, it is possible exercising some influence for good over our lives ; at all events, the loss is only on our side, and that for a short time : so that I cannot talk of poor Tom, or call the news sad—I only feel the very earthly feeling of regret that when I get back I shall not see his dear kind old face, or hear his favourite greeting, into which he used to throw so much love and interest, of ' Well, boy !' The very feeling which will perhaps make the tears come into your eyes as you read this, as they have into mine as I write, only shows what a softening influence love is, and what a beautifying effect it would have on our lives if we could feel more universally for our fellow-creatures what we feel for Tom."

In a similar way he discusses the feeling of thankfulness for his escape from drowning, of which he tells her :—

"As far as you are concerned, I often think if I have a narrow shave that it is perfectly legitimate the feeling should be one of thankfulness. I should feel the same about you, but not about myself. The reason I feel it about you, and you about me, is because we are both selfish in respect to one another; but thankfulness on the part of the individual himself at being saved from death seems to me the most wretched mundane sentiment possible, to say nothing of its being dishonouring to God. If we are always thankful for being kept alive, it is very evident that we must regard His dispensation of death as a hardship to be disgusted with whenever it comes. As if He were not to be trusted to keep us in this world or send us to the next in His own good time! I am not in the least a fatalist : I should struggle in the water to the last gasp; but when it did come, as I feel now, I should be perfectly satisfied. I have the most unbounded confidence in the universal economy of things, and I don't like implying that God could be guilty of an act of caprice or injustice by being thankful for His sparing me,

when, if He did not, I should not be entitled
to complain."

Nothing can be more interesting than these
indications of the way in which the thoughts of
the young man, amid surroundings so little congenial to any prolonged process of thinking, were
occupied. It would be vain to pretend that they
were either original or profound ; indeed they are
throughout pervaded by the curious confusion
between Christianity as a religious system and
the shortcomings of its professors,—as if it were
incumbent upon a thinking man to abjure the
faith in order to protest against the faults of
those who failed to obey it, which we have
already pointed out. But they are interesting
as showing how early and how independently the
germs which were so to develop in after-life had
gained possession of his mind. His views upon .
that inspiration, which was the same as intuition,
and the consequent subjection of every actual
truth to the feeling and instinct of the believer ;
his determination that every influence should
be judged according to its practical power over
himself—even his views in respect to the parting
of death, and the attitude we ought to hold towards it,—are all germs of the faith which afterwards led him to so many singular steps. They

are interesting in this respect as well as for themselves,—unusual matter to occupy the mind of a young man in his circumstances. He was approaching his twenty-ninth birthday, and his life hitherto had been one of almost wild adventure, continual movement, and restless occupation.

On the other hand, however, there was plenty of adventure to record. He took a share in everything, whatever was going on. When a flag of truce was sent up the Canton river with Lord Elgin's ultimatum, he volunteered, as has been said, for the duty; and though he agreed that it was better left in the hands of Wade, who was a Chinese scholar, than in his own, yet he "begged hard," as he says, to have the errand. When Captain Sherard Osborn went off in the Furious to Manilla, Laurence got permission to accompany him, to vary the monotony of the long waiting at Hong-Kong; but here a difficulty arose. "Sherard Osborn," he writes, "is the fellow whom I pitched into so furiously at the Geographical about the Sea of Azoff, so I may not get him to take me;" but Captain Osborn was magnanimous, and did not recall this old score. The most amusing thing in the journey is the description of High Mass in the cathedral at Manilla, which "was a most grotesque performance."

" The troops marched into church, filling nearly
the whole of it, and six men with swords drawn
took up a position on the altar platform to
present arms to the priest. The band was
immediately below this, and opened proceedings
with a very pretty *deux - temps* waltz. They
principally played polkas and waltzes, sometimes
kneeling, sometimes standing,—the men crossing
themselves in quick time, making a sort of polka
step on their faces with wonderful rapidity. I
tried crossing myself in quick time, but made a
mess of it. The whole thing lasted about half
an hour, and consisted entirely of music. The
officiating priest was a black man, who never said
anything, and only occasionally elevated the
Host, and turned round to bless the congregation
in pantomime."

After long inaction and various attempts at
negotiation, the united forces found themselves
compelled to proceed to the bombardment of
Canton, which was taken with the greatest of
ease and the utmost rapidity, scarcely any resistance being made. Laurence and some of the
other non - combatants watched the proceedings
from an eminence close by, on a hill used as a
cemetery, where they found " shelter from the
flying balls in a deep little grave." " Un-

fortunately," he says, "the very imperfection of their modes of defence is the greatest danger in Chinese warfare. If you are alone in the midst of a silent turnip - field, you are as likely to be hit as if you were immediately under the walls with an attacking party, for they have no idea of taking aim, and their rockets go shying about in all conceivable directions." He had seen "a brave young fellow killed by one of these wild projectiles within five or six yards of him," but still it was difficult to believe there was any danger, they were so few and far between.

"This sort of thing went on until half-past eight, when the Braves made an attack on our extreme right, of which we had a capital view; but we were soon diverted from looking at this by the cheers in front, and we saw the scaling-ladders up, and our fellows clustering like bees into a hive. We immediately bolted down to join them, and in five minutes stood upon the city wall, deserted by every vestige of a Chinaman, except those that were lying dead along the parapet. We had a magnificent view of the vast city, with its million of inhabitants, at our feet, not showing a sign of life. Not a living creature was to be seen throughout its whole extent. The streets, to be sure, are so narrow that you can't see far into them ; but when you did, you only saw dead or occasionally wounded people. I went down with the General to the other end of the wall, a mile and a half distant, where they were potting at our fellows from the tops of houses, and while I was there poor Bower of the 59th was wounded—I fear mortally. However, it was their last effort. We made this our advanced post in this direction. I wanted to get back with all my news to Lord Elgin. I took advantage of a party going to open up a new communication, got down to the river, and was on board the Furious in time, as you know, to catch the post by about five minutes."

He defends himself some time later, when he has had time to receive letters from home blaming him for thus unnecessarily exposing himself at Canton, in an amusing way. He was wrong, he allows. " But it involves a greater act of self-denial than any I know to refrain from going to see anything approaching to a fight. And though in principle I utterly disapprove of war, when it comes to 'Away there, second cutters !' human nature can't resist jumping in, whatever good resolutions one may have formed to the contrary."

It is unnecessary to follow the course of the expedition, which was still exposed to extraordinary delays, even after this apparently decisive step. Laurence cannot refrain from a temptation still greater than that of warfare — a little abuse of the spirit of revenge, which he found so strongly developed among so-called religious persons. He tells his mother that the missionaries at Shanghai, where the expedition went after reducing Canton to the most prostrate subjection, were revolted by the mildness of Lord Elgin's measures. "Like Lord Shaftesbury, they are truly English, and grumble at our not having murdered Yeh and given Canton over to pillage and slaughter. As a general rule, one thinks that justice ought to be tempered with mercy; but they would have vengeance tempered with justice!" It is well to add, however, that the "parson with a Crimean medal pinned on his surplice," who had made him angry by preaching on hell, turned out "a very nice fellow" when they watched Canton together from among the tombs. But Laurence was little favourable to missionaries in general, and felt with many others that the good incomes, good houses, and worldly comfort of men who were supposed to be sacrificing everything for Christ's work, were jarring circumstances, to say the

least. His comparison between the Jesuit schools
at Shanghai and those of the Protestant missionaries was perhaps touched with the same
prejudice, yet no doubt had truth in it.   Of
the first, he says :—

"I was struck with the intelligent expression
of the youths' countenances, and the apparent
affection they had for their teachers. Instead
of cramming nothing but texts down their
throats, they teach them the Chinese classics,
Confucius, &c., so as to enable them to compete
in the examinations. The result is, that even
if they do not become Christians, they have always gratitude enough to protect those to whom
they owed their education, and perhaps consequent rise in life. I also went over a school
with the Bishop. The contrast was most striking. Small boys gabbled the Creed over in
what was supposed to be English ; but in one
instance Lord Elgin was profoundly persuaded
it was Chinese. They understood probably about
as clearly as they pronounced. Then, instead of
the missionaries living among them and identify-
ing themselves with the boys, they have gorgeous houses, wives, and families. A missionary
here with a wife and four children gets a house
as big as Spring Grove rent free, and £500

a-year : and that is called giving up all for the
sake of the heathen !"

The difficulties under which the expedition had
to be carried out throw a curious light upon the
hindrances, unsuspected by the general public, to
which even the most important public work is
exposed. Thus between two and three months
were lost at Hong-Kong, while the forces sent out
from England to replace those carried off to India
were on the way. And again, at the mouth of
the Peiho the whole mission was arrested for a
month by the blunder or obstinacy of the
admirals, who would not furnish gunboats which
could cross the bar and ascend the river. I may
quote one amusing incident of the subjection of
the town of Tientsin, in which the private narrative of the letters is even more picturesque
than that afterwards published. The town had
capitulated, but was unfriendly and apt to do
or say something disagreeable when occasion
served. Thus two of the captains of the fleet
were insulted on a visit they paid, without escort
or alarm, to some of the shops and streets. A
detachment of a hundred marines was sent to
punish the offenders, but on reaching the town
found the gates closed against them. Laurence,
generally to be found by some lucky accident

wherever anything was going on, had accompanied them on horseback.

"Osborn and I, however, discovered a scalable place where a house was built against the wall; so we took three blue-jackets, and with Drew got on the roof and thus scrambled on to the wall, the bricks being decayed so as to give us something to hold to. Then with bayonets and revolvers drawn we rushed down with a frantic yell upon the unsuspecting crowd collected at the gate, thinking they had succeeded in barring us out. They took to their heels, struck to a panic by the six barbarians, and we smashed the bar of the gate and let the warriors in, with whom we paraded the town, making six prisoners at the place where the outrage was committed."

The commissioners from the Emperor, obtained after much difficulty to settle the treaty, which for the first time admitted foreign traders, as a right, to the Celestial Empire, met Lord Elgin at this town,—Laurence in the meanwhile having been much occupied in "collecting from old treaties and other sources all the points" that could be employed in the new. The other special missions upon which Laurence was himself engaged—such as that to Soochow, Nankin, and some others—are fully recorded in his book. The private narrative adds little, except on the former occasion an account of his troubles with a vapouring French consul, who was the adviser of his colleague the French secretary, but exceedingly unpopular as well as injudicious. Having achieved the treaty, the expedition went to Japan, returning to Shanghai and Canton for the final ratification. In the hurried and brief visit to Japan there was nothing but pleasurable excitement before them,—the first discovery, so to speak, of a wonderful new nation, the wonder and enigma of modern times. In the second volume of Laurence's 'Narrative' there will be found full details of this visit; but in his letters it has very little space, partly, I think, because, like all the rest of the mission, he had become very tired of his banishment, and in the hope of a speedy return home put off his descriptions of the unknown country till he should be able to give them by word of mouth. "We were all enchanted with Japan," he says, writing from Shanghai on their return.

"*Sept.* 1, 1858.

"At Sinoden we heard from the American consul that in consequence of the moral effect of our having forced the Chinamen into a treaty, he had just been able to conclude one at Yeddo; so we proceeded there, and the Japanese saw for the first time in their lives four foreign ships anchor off the capital. They were most civil, and gave us a capital lodging on shore in a temple. Six commissioners were appointed to treat, and I never ceased regretting that you had prevented me from learning Dutch at the Cape in consideration of my morals, though I daresay I should have forgotten it—as it was the only medium of communication here, and we had to make use of the American interpreter. I had a considerable finger in the pie nevertheless, Lord Elgin very kindly letting me take as prominent a place as circumstances would permit. The commissioners were capital fellows, and so different from the Chinese, so full of animation and life, and very go-ahead. They are the most good - tempered people I ever met, and Japan is the only country I was ever in where there is no poverty and beggars are unknown. Much as I should hate going to China in any capacity, I would willingly go to Japan, and I am sure, were I to get the appointment of Consul-General there, you and papa would like it. Of course all this has furnished me with plenty of material for my book."

His mind, it must be added, was at this mo

ment, as the work of the mission was nearly over,
again much occupied by thoughts of a permanent
appointment.   One of those which were spoken of
was the appointment of Governor of the Straits
Settlements, to which he was inclined ; but it is
evident that he would gladly have accepted any
fitting post in his anxiety to attain a settled position in life.   To be Secretary of Legation at a
foreign capital would have been in some respects
still more congenial.   A wife, which he had for
years decided half in jest and half in earnest to
be the first necessity of all, is also spoken of.   On
the other hand, " 1 sometimes think I will throw
up all my present ambitions, try and find some
one with three or four hundred a-year, and settle
down in a small way at a European capital to
work out my own problems.   After all," he adds,
" there is no such happiness as living in one's own
world of thought.   At present my thoughts run
on aniseed, almonds, beans, *bêche de mer*, and so
on through all the tariff.   What ennobling and
elevating subjects for contemplation !"   At the
moment when he thus expressed himself, he was
discussing point by point with the Chinese Commissioners the details of duties and imports, and
very weary of his work.

The snatches of gaiety which broke the routine
of tedious life furnish some amusing incidents to

the narrative, but very often are weighted with a moral, and many assaults upon the manners of the mercantile communities. At one place the ball came to its conclusion in an effective surprise. " Lord Elgin and I finished with a reel for the edification of the public, took a tender farewell of society, and embarked during the small hours of the morning, so that when the world awoke next day we were no more to be seen." At another place the company was *dévote*, and a different kind of entertainment was necessary.

" The King of Denmark's fiddler has been here, and we had music and singing for Mrs M. and other non-dancing ladies; but when they left we danced till a late hour. Lord Elgin stumped Mrs M. by asking if that were not the time for dancing mentioned by Solomon, and what hour of the day she thought he would approve? She denied that he said there was a time for dancing, but has since found chapter and verse, and has given in, but evidently thinks Solomon was wrong. The Bishop and his wife are becoming dabs at billiards; but the other night when the missionaries were dining he would not allow the billiard-room to be lighted, though he is generally the last to leave it. Woe unto you Evangelists and Puseyites, hypocrites! To abstain from dancing, and

love to be seen in fine bonnets at church, and at
the head of subscription lists ostentatiously [here
follows a long tirade]. . . . There is a sudden
explosion for you, which has taken me as much by
surprise as you. Poor Bishop! I don't mean to
abuse him. I think by the way he button-holes
me, and talks confidential platitudes to me in
corners, that he rather likes me. He constantly
excuses the missionaries for going into the country
against treaty, &c., though I carefully refrain from
reflecting on them; so I suppose it is his own conscience. I believe he is a good man. He confirms
to-day a lot of middies who have been prepared
for the ceremony by our convivial parson, and who,
though nice young fellows, are some of them such
scamps that their sponsors must be immensely
relieved by the load that will be lifted from
their shoulders."

Laurence is never happier than when he sends
a flying shaft thus at the " worldly holy," against
whom afterwards, in ' Piccadilly,' he poured forth
his keenest satire. He tells his mother afterwards that he had nearly embroiled himself with
the lady mentioned above, for laughing at a
society for Biblical discussion among the ladies,
one member of which had distinguished Bishop
Heber as a descendant of Heber the Kenite. " I

said that as a lawyer I was superior to all clergy as an interpreter of texts, and suggested that I should be elected permanent referee to the ladies— with other foolish nonsense," he writes, repentant, having made his peace. But the society of these seaports, " worse than a colony," as he says, grew more and more intolerable to him as the days lingered on. " The men think of nothing but tea, silk, and opium ; the women are too apathetic to care even for gaiety and crinoline. We are going to make a spasmodic attempt to amuse them with a ball ; but Fitzroy is in despair, for only eight ladies have accepted and 120 men ! "

Meanwhile his metaphysical thinkings and readings go on, and he has a mingled disappointment and delight in finding the metaphysical and religious work he had intended to produce forestalled by Mr William Smith's ' Thorndale,' in which he has been " revelling," and which " represents my own ideas and condition of mind better than anything I could myself give." " Mind you read every word of it to papa," he repeats, " and think over it the while, and of me, when you read the chapter called ' Childhood,' as I did of you."

He is afterwards astonished and delighted, " after what I wrote to you about ' Thorndale,' that just as I should be making you a present of a copy of it, I should receive one with your dear handwriting on the title-page!" Another book which he had read with pleasure was a very different one, Miss Marsh's 'Hearts and Hands,' an account of her mission among the navvies. He wonders, not unnaturally, whether his complicated religious system would have any influence upon such people; but comforts himself by the thought that a complicated system need not be less true than a simpler one, and that those who act by reason are less likely to be backsliders than those who are moved by enthusiasm. Their progress may be slow, but it is sure.

"In my own case it is awfully slow; but then consider the difficulty of having to build away for one's self and fight against prejudice existing in every form around, and compare my condition with that of the worldly man who becomes a 'converted Christian.' He flings himself at once into the religious world, where he is supported and taught and cared for, his difficulties explained and his faith strengthened, and sails smoothly and easily down the stream. To put it in the form of an equation, he is to me as is a Roman Catholic to him. He thinks the Roman Catholic has his religion done for him, I think the Protestant has his religion done for him. So different is religion in these days from what it was in the days of Christ, that the worldly man does not persecute the saint, but the saint persecutes the worldly man. It requires infinitely more strength of mind and moral courage to come out from the religious world and to be separate, than to come out from the worldly one."

This perpetual assault against the religious world may be explained by the fact that the exterior conventionalities of that world had been more or less always present, overshadowing his life, until the young man emancipated himself from them. It would have been perhaps more wonderful had he lived to perceive nowadays that in many circles the greatest courage and strength of mind is required from those who profess any belief at all. He defends himself once more from the accusation of "setting up his reason," which his mother had brought against him.

"You must remember that the fact that we believe many things we don't understand does not prove that when we don't understand a thing we should believe it. We have only our reason to decide for us the cases in which it voluntarily allows itself to be suspended. It preaches faith equally in your case as in mine, only I require stronger grounds to influence me than you do. But I think that it is a mistake to hold on to it too long. I have long since taken refuge in my intuitions."

Reason, tempered by intuition, was thus the rule to which he had attained, alone and without spiritual guidance of any kind. The reader will perceive that thus the doors of his heart were wide open, so that any interpreter who commended himself, if that were possible, to both, might enter in.

His return home after this, the longest absence from his parents which he had ever undergone, was a very mournful one. For the dear "Papa," whom he rarely called by any but that tender childish title, died suddenly a short time before the expedition came back. It was, I think, at one of the ports of Ceylon—a place so associated with him — that Laurence received the news. Sir Anthony's death was entirely unexpected, and occurred, I believe, at a dinner-party to which he had gone in his usual health. I have been told that, being at sea at the time, Laurence came on deck one morning and informed his comrades that he had seen his father in the night, and that he was dead — that they en-

deavoured to laugh him out of the impression,
but in vain. The date was taken down, and
on their arrival in England it was found that
Sir Anthony Oliphant had indeed died on that
night—which would be a remarkable addition,
if sufficiently confirmed, to many stories of a
similar kind which are well known. He always
appears in his son's letters and in his wife's
in the most engaging light — a cheerful and
bright spirit interested in everything about
him, as curious of novelty and excitement as
his own son was, delighting to find himself
in the heart of everything that was going
on. The jokes about " the darling," in which
he indulged in the earlier Colombo days, half
hiding under a humorous pretence at jealousy
the delight and pride in the beloved boy, which
he felt as warmly as the mother did, and his
readiness to follow Lowry wherever his fortunes
led him, are as lovable and delightful as is the
confidence of Laurence in papa's comprehension
and sympathy and the charm of his companionship. The mother and son discuss him indeed
sometimes as mothers and children will do, as if
he were a big schoolboy, whose pranks are charming, but whose health and comfort has to be
looked after by more careful heads than his own ;
but in his judgment on serious matters his son

had always the fullest reliance, and the highest testimony his wife could give to the excellence of the new tenets she adopted in later days was that "our beloved Sir Anthony" would have found comfort in them.

He would not seem, however, to have exercised much guidance, but rather to have allowed himself genially to follow where his boy's erratic steps led — now to the Crimea, now to the Stirling burghs, where papa's electioneering was most lively and active. The only "No" which seems ever recorded of him is when Laurence, young and sanguine, made a demand for money to invest in America—to which Sir Anthony replied with the dry but admirable advice that his son should save anything he could from his official salary and invest that. This advice was so far taken that Laurence became the possessor of "a town lot" in the city of Superior, of which he afterwards made the admirable use of establishing upon it a friend who was under the shadow of severe misfortune, and for whom a refuge was thus obtained. It brought in, however, save in this way, no profit to its proprietor.

Sir Anthony's death made the union between mother and son more close and all-absorbing than ever ; but it did not bind the active and restless young man to England, a result for which his spirit of adventure is not alone to be blamed. For he neglected no effort to establish himself in the diplomatic service nearer home, and it is evident that it was the prick of injured feeling, the sickness at heart of continual disappointment, the spurns which patient merit has to accept, if not of the unworthy, at least of the official world, which drove him again and again from England. It was indeed impatient merit in Oliphant's case. He would not wait kicking his heels outside the doors of the Colonial or Foreign Office. It was a necessity with him to be doing, if not one thing then another. Both his active temperament and the state of his mind in respect to religious and other matters fomented this impatience. He explains it to his mother by the following excellent reasons, while also apologising to her for not writing of his "interior," which was what she always most desired :—

"So long as I have anything to interest me, I keep myself so fully occupied and usefully employed that time passes pleasantly and profitably, and I do not compromise myself; but when I have nothing to do except to be consistent in hours of temptation which are constantly recurring, and have no employment to absorb me, I go with the stream, having an utter want of self-denial. I find the only substitute is occupation, and that I cannot have on circuit, as it must be engrossing, which law is not. The consequence is, that I am in low spirits unless I am actively engaged."

It is characteristic of his breeding and the perpetual self-examinations to which he had been made to subject himself, modified into a curiously unusual vein by the originality of his own mind, that he should go on from this into a lament over the incongruity of his mental and moral position :

" I find it impossible to divest my conversation and conduct of that frivolity which marks the worldly mind, and which gives the lie to any sudden outburst of morality I may think it necessary to assume. Nobody could conceive how deeply I feel the reality and truth of religion from my conduct, considering the force of my convictions and the occasional earnestness of my prayers. In days when I was almost insensible to religion of any sort, or had any principle except my love for you, I was infinitely less capable of evil than I am now; but now that I begin to delight in the love of God after the inward man, the law of my members seems moved into activity. As this said law always gets the best of it, you will perceive that I must be harassed in proportion as the struggle is great. However, I could go on theorising for hours; and now that I come to read it over, I daresay it is all humbug from beginning to end, and that is another reason why I don't like writing this sort of stuff. How am I ever to be satisfied, after analysing my feelings, that I am right? It seems to me one of the most fruitless occupations in the world. It does not appear to me that the human mind is endowed with faculties adequate to the task. It instinctively knows its own weakness, but it is not competent to say where that weakness lies or how it may be cured, or else it would be competent to cure it, which it certainly is not. If a divine power is necessary to overcome the depravity of one's human nature, a divine revelation is necessary to enable one to discern wherein that depravity precisely consists. Therefore, as I said before, I may be all wrong, with which consideration you must comfort yourself; also with feeling that I have relieved my mind by writing all this, whether it is nonsense or not."

One cannot but feel a half-amused sympathy for the mother, thus tantalised by revelations in which there was so much which must have satisfied her craving for information respecting her son's innermost thoughts, and so much that must have puzzled and confounded her. How far did the boy mean what he said? and how far was it humbug, as he says? All the pages of theorising which he addressed to her—his bold criticisms of the things she reverenced most, and breakings-off into new paths—never, however, discouraged her; until the time came when they both beheld the new light, as it seemed to them, together, and all qualms on the one side and uncertainties on the other were swept away.

After his two years' service in China, it was natural to suppose that his hopes of definite and permanent employment would have been realised; but either the Foreign Office did not think so, or its slowness of operation and prejudice in favour of those who had entered its service in the usual way made its authorities impervious to the claims of the brilliant young interloper, who had, though so successful and valuable a public servant, leaped into the service rather by private favour of a friendly plenipotentiary than in the legitimate way. At all events, he had got tired of waiting by the end of the year, and in the early beginning of 1860 we find him plunged into a new excitement. Probably he had remained more or less a sympathiser with Italy since the time when he took a delighted share in all the mischief going on, a dozen years before, when he was a boy travelling with his parents; but there is no indication to show us what it was which made him suppose that he could do something to stay the course of events, when just at the crisis of the fate of Nice and Savoy he rushed out of London and threw himself into the excitement of Italian politics in Turin—where the cession was being reluctantly carried through—and Nice, where he actually hoped to have reversed the order of things, and roused the languid population to resistance. It is curious to find him discussing sentimental methods and quoting the ' Biglow Papers': " I don't believe in principle, but oh I du in interest!" in respect to national action, while setting out on the most romantic piece of knight-errantry in his own person. His journey to Nice and Turin had, of course, two aspects; and he scarcely discloses even in his delightful after-narrative, published when all necessity for secrecy was over, the daring hope he had of becoming himself an important agent in the matter, and perhaps saving the provinces which Italy, not yet consolidated into a great nation, was compelled to sacrifice to her great and noble aim. To ordinary eyes it was pure love of adventure, tempered by the pursuit of " copy " and

material for articles, chiefly in 'Blackwood,' which
carried him forth; and he is profuse in his explanations to his mother that the fifty pounds
he would make by two articles was quite justification enough for the brief crusade, lasting only
a month, upon which he set out in high hopes.

Leaving Paris, Laurence found himself, to his
great annoyance, yet amusement, in the same
carriage "with some frowsy parties enveloped in
tobacco-smoke," who turned out to be the very
deputies from Nice, returning from their interview with the Emperor, whom he was bent on
overcoming; but with whom he became so friendly,
picking their brains of any political secrets to be
found there, that he was taken for one of them
by an official who came to the railway to pay
his respects to the deputation. "He made me
a low bow, which I returned with all the dignity
becoming a man who has just sold his country."
In Savoy he found enough of patriotic feeling
and smouldering undirected enthusiasm to fill
him with high hopes; and his first resolution,
after egging up these local patriots to resistance,
was to write letters to every member of the Parliament in Turin, urging them to delay the ratification of the treaty,—a tremendous step to be
taken by a young man on his own responsibility.
His earnestness and conviction that something

might actually be done in this way was not
unmingled with levity. "It is great fun," he
writes, "to have another object than churches
and picture-galleries;" but he was not the less
seriously disappointed and humiliated when he
found that things had gone too far, and that all
his eloquence, excitement, and inspiration could
not produce the effects he had desired.

His acquaintance with diplomatic society carried
him at once to the heart of affairs in Turin, and
made him acquainted with all the now historical
details of that great era in Italian history. He
met and dined with Cavour, whom he describes as
"a thick-set solid man, with a large square head
and spectacles, an able, mathematical, practical
sort of head, without chivalry, principle, or genius,"
—a harsh judgment, which he afterwards saw cause
to alter. But his chief interest was Garibaldi, by
whose aid alone any operation like that of which
he dreamed was practicable. The impatience of
the young man, used to constitutional methods,
and conscious of the efficacy of popular agitation,
with the still bewildered patriots, who were quite
unable to employ such new tools, is characteristic.

"Why I should take such intense interest in
affairs that don't concern me I don't know, except
that I cannot stand by and see a good cause ruined,

and such blackguards as the Emperor carrying all before him, without wagging a finger. And these people, with all their patriotism, are so childish and unpractical, Garibaldi worst of all. I have got him regularly in tow, but cannot din the only practicable plan for the salvation of his country into his head. He is the most amiable, innocent, honest nature possible, and a first-rate guerilla chief, but in council a child. The worst of him is that he puts his trust in anybody, and unless you stick to him you lose your influence; but he has a name with the people that may be turned to any account."

The zeal of the young self-sent emissary seems to have been able to inspirit the drooping party of disconsolate Nizzards so far as to procure the proposal of a resolution against the annexation, in Parliament, by Garibaldi, Laurence himself drawing it out. But "it is of no use, I feel certain," he says; "they can neither work popular movements nor parliamentary tactics." That the malcontents should never have thought of calling a public meeting at Nice, where the people might have expressed their feelings, fills him with indignant astonishment. Failing these constitutional methods, remained the romantic one of seizing and breaking the ballot-boxes when the votes were collected, so as to make another ballot necessary, and thus gain a little time, which would seem to have been fully planned by the energetic young revolutionary. But this promising plan was abandoned by the distraction of Garibaldi's thoughts toward Sicily, as may be seen in the 'Episodes.' The young man promises to his mother to "keep out of the row"; but we know what such undertakings come to in the case of an individual who had confessed that it was beyond human nature to hear that a fight was going on, and not rush out to see it. And what the Foreign Office would have thought of a possible Secretary of Legation breaking the ballot-boxes at the head of a party of Garibaldian red-shirts it would not be difficult to predict. Thus, perhaps, according to his prevailing conviction, it was all for the best that he should have been compelled to add, in deep disappointment, "There is not the slightest chance of a row—the people are like sheep."

"The business here has gone off with the usual flatness. Still I am glad to have seen it, and to have known the villanies that have been perpetrated under the pretext of universal suffrage. The whole thing was a sham of the most transparent character. A popular leader like Garibaldi ought to have turned the tables. A little

more of Walker in his composition would have
settled the matter." Always philosophical, however, and remembering now that the affairs of
Italy did not really concern him in the least,
Laurence consoled himself by thoughts of the
pounds which would be brought in by two articles
in 'Blackwood,' which were more than his expedition had cost him altogether.

He seems to have travelled much this year,
since we hear of him two or three months later
in Montenegro, where various amusing incidents
happened to him, related in the 'Episodes'; and
after that in Naples, where he was once more
received by Garibaldi, by that time victor of
Sicily, and about to round out the new-formed
Italian kingdom by the magnificent present of
the ancient Regno, the only royal state in the
peninsula. Laurence relates that he was accom-
modated on this occasion in the very palace and
bedchamber of King Bomba himself, " in a bed
so gorgeous with its gold and lace and satin, that
I doubted whether the king himself did not keep
it for show. However, it turned out a very good
one to sleep in," adds the light-hearted traveller,
whose next night's rest might be in a brigand's
hut or in the close little cabin of a felucca, for
anything he knew or cared.

It was in one more out of the way still, in the

paper chamber of a Japanese temple, that for almost
the first time in all his adventurous career we find
him in absolute peril of his life.   Notwithstanding
what seems at the first glance the rapid advance
and invariable success of his life, Laurence had
not been as yet, as I have already had occasion to
remark, distinguished by Government patronage.
When the appointment as First Secretary of
Legation at Japan was offered to him, it was thus
a most important step in his career : though possibly, as it was to replace a gentleman murdered
barbarously in China, and involved danger to life
as well as a very distant exile out of the world,
it was not eagerly sought after by the usual candidates.   To Laurence, however, whose experiences of Japan in his former brief visit with
Lord Elgin—when all was novel and fresh, and
the strangers were received with *naïve* enthusiasm before any complications had arisen—were
all delightful, the offer, as he says, was " extremely tempting," especially as it was in reality
the first really official appointment which he had
held.   He arrived in Yedo (I adopt his own spel-
ling of the word) in the end of June 1861, the
Minister, Sir Rutherford Alcock, then Mr Alcock,
being at the time absent, which constituted
Laurence for the time being *chargé d'affaires*.
His usual correspondence with his mother here

unfortunately fails me; but I am permitted to quote from a letter addressed to the Duchess of Somerset, which gives a very vivid representation of the state of affairs, and shows the changed condition of the Japanese mind towards the powerful invaders whom they had previously received with so much cordiality. This letter was written only a few days before the outrage which so completely changed his prospects.

"YEDO, *July* 2 [1861].

"I am at present luxuriating in that feeling of repose which arises from having arrived at one's journey's end, and am agreeably surprised with the aspect of my future abode. Mr Alcock is still away, so that I found myself *locum tenens* immediately on my arrival. The important questions which are pending are of course left over until his return, and things are going on quietly enough, in so far as one's personal safety is concerned. That we shall have ultimately to join issue with the Japanese no one can doubt who watches for a moment the tone of their diplomacy; but I shall be able to write to you at more length upon that subject when I have been here a little longer. We expect the Admiral in a week or ten days, and I trust that when he comes he will see the expediency of keeping a large force in these parts. At present we have only one despatch gunboat for the whole of Japan. So far as we are concerned here, with a due amount of prudence and submission to Government restraint, there is no reason why any disturbance should arise; but at Yokohama, only seventeen miles off, there are upwards of a hundred Europeans, and their patience under the galling restraints to which they are subjected cannot always be counted upon.

" I can imagine few places of residence more delightful than this, if that one all-pervading drawback of Government surveillance were removed. In fact, a State prisoner would consider himself in clover, but a free-born Briton cannot regard matters in the same light. At Yokohama these restraints are much mitigated, and people may ride and walk where they like unattended; but we here are never for a moment unwatched. The beauty of our pleasure-grounds, which consist of twenty or thirty acres of garden, wood, and water, is quite destroyed by the fact of three hundred guards being posted in them. If my servant runs after a butterfly, a two-sworded official runs after him; and one post completely commands my rooms, so that my every act is noticed. As the whole is enclosed by a palisade, every gate is guarded. We are never attended by less than eight when we go out; these scramble over the country after us, and prohibit our stopping to speak to the people, much more to shop in the town. Indeed there is no inducement to go into the town after one is familiar with it, as the streets are crowded and the chances of collision greater. As a general rule, our guardians exercise their functions with civility. When they are impertinent, as sometimes happens, one has to submit as one would to one's jailer. All this is rather trying, and is a useful exercise of temper.

"It is due to Mr Alcock to say that his retirement to Kanogan produced a good effect, though it was a bold stroke, as, if the Government had not yielded, there was no escape from the dilemma. Practically one is perfectly safe if one is prudent, submits to discipline, and is respectful in one's bearing when one meets the native grandees or their retainers. For instance, on a narrow path the Englishman, if he desires to avoid a collision, makes way for the grandee's servant. Then there is no occasion to go out after dark, or to resent insulting expressions from intoxicated Yacomins. With entire humility one is in no danger whatever, and a truly sincere Christian who exercised the highest of Christian graces might live here in perfect safety all his life. All my old friends have disappeared from the scene. One, who was an especial favourite

of mine when I was here last, ripped himself up
a short time ago ; and two of the other commissioners are disgraced, and it is supposed have
followed his example.   This was all on account
of their friendship for foreigners.   A man told me
that he was struck by the subdued expression of
my friend's countenance the other day when he
went to see him ; but he had no suspicion that
that high-spirited individual intended to put an
end to himself.   He had, in fact, already sent out
cards of invitation for a ' happy despatch ' party,
and at the most jovial moment of the banquet
he addressed his friends in a few telling words,
and vindicated his honour in their presence.

" Every one, down to the lowest interpreter, who
has had anything to do with the introduction
of the foreigners, has disappeared or been disgraced, and the hostile nobles do not hesitate to
say that they are only waiting till they are better
drilled and organised to go to war with us.   In
fact, they pay us the compliment of saying that
we are the only nation they can go to war with,
as we are the only nation from whom they can
learn anything."

This state of affairs was evidently an impossible
one to last ; but its conclusion, so far as Oliphant
was concerned, though most alarming and nearly

tragical, was not a public outrage, but one that might have happened in any unsettled country, the work of a handful of unauthorised ruffians; and the guard, whose inquisition was so intolerable to the gentlemen cooped up in the lodging which was thus made into a prison, seem to have defended them faithfully at the cost of several lives. The attack, which was of the most highly dramatic character, is perhaps one of the best known incidents in Oliphant's life. He has described it in the most vivid manner in his 'Episodes': and the letter in which he communicated the event to his mother, though with a few characteristic and individual touches of private sentiment, differs little from the after-narrative, and bears marks in its broken sentences and hurried contractions of the difficulty with which he still wrote. He had been only about a week in discharge of his functions, and had just been relieved of his responsibility as chief of the embassy by the arrival of Mr Alcock, when one night, having sat late to look at a comet, most fortunately, as it happened, Laurence was startled by various sounds,—the barking of a dog which he had attached to himself by kindness (which was a way he had with dogs as well as men), and which slept at his door, the sound of the rattle used by the Japanese watchmen, and other suspicious noises. Jumping up in the dark, he could find no weapon handy but a hunting-crop with a heavily weighted handle, with which he rushed out into the narrow passage on which his room opened, calling several members of the legation as he went.

"Just as I turned the corner I came upon a tall black figure, with his arms above his head, holding a huge two-handed sword. As the only light came round the corner from R.'s room, I could only see indistinctly that the figure had a mask on, and seemed in armour. Short time for observation, had to dodge the sword, and get back a step to get at him with my whip, yelling loudly. It seemed like a nightmare, meeting a huge black figure coming in the night into your house to take stealthily your blood, whom you had never harmed. He made no sound: we were at it for a minute or two. I could not hope to do him much harm: my only object was to keep him at bay until somebody came; nobody did. I soon got a cut in the right shoulder, and then managed to entangle his sword in the handle of the whip—it has the marks. I could not see his blows, as it was dark; but at length one came down on my left arm, which I instinctively had kept over my head as a guard.

At the same moment Morison, who had time to load a pistol, opened his door and fired. The man dropped, but another fellow rushed at Morison and cut him over the head; then both got back round the corner, the man on the ground only floored, the other fatally wounded. Morison and I retired."

This is the first breathless account of the sudden fight in the dark. When the two wounded men fell back on the room in which two or three of their fellows were now gathered after a hurried search for arms, and in which there was a feeble light, an interval of terrible suspense occurred. Bligh, Oliphant's servant, had dashed through the paper partition of his room, to join the party with his double-barrelled gun : all the arms that could be mustered besides were two revolvers and a sword, and with these means of defence, paper walls and screens their only shelter, and two wounded men to hinder any escape, the little group stood listening for the renewed attack. Fortunately, however, the guards outside were faithful, and the assassins were successfully driven back, although fighting went on during the whole course of the anxious night. Next day Laurence, whose wounds had been bound up by Mr Alcock, was conveyed to the gunboat in the harbour, the Ringdove, "escorted by Alcock and whole mission, file of blue-jackets, second of Yacomins, all armed to teeth, a most pic. procession," writes the sufferer, his eyes open under all circumstances. " One's collar-bone sewn up prevents use of right arm yet ; other hurts are left arm, two cuts above wrist. Doctors promise better in three weeks." This was scribbled on the 10th of July, four days after the event. On the 11th he goes on : " Better : first three days both arms had to be strapped across chest. Bligh fed me and nursed me in the tenderest manner ; but I alone here, captain and men on shore. Sleeping on back, with thermometer at 85°, trussed like a fowl, is difficult, but we are jolly." After some discussion of the position, the following note is added at the end :—

" My only thought that night was for you : for myself I am glad ; it made me know I could face death, which at one time seemed inevitable. I found my creed or philosophy quite satisfactory. I take everything as in the day's work, and that is why in one sense I do not feel thankful like others. I have such a profound feeling of being in God's hands, and having nothing to do with my own fate, that gratitude even would be presumption. If killed, I have no doubt my first feel-

ing in the other world would be one of relief; just
as my first feeling at not being killed was one of
relief too.   It seems to me to make no difference :
whatever is, is best ; and I feel I could realise this
amid considerable pain.   Since wounded do not
wish to complain ; acquiescence during short stay
here no great heroism.   I do not know that I
should say so always ; but as yet I can, and I see
it is the right thing.   It must all end ; one has
only to hold on, and feel sure that the use and
object of it all will be evident.   Meantime to do
the right thing :

> Live I, so live I
> To my Lord heartily,
> To my Prince faithfully,
> To my neighbour honestly,
> Die I, so die I.

"If God is good, it must all come right in the
end.   I never doubt Him.   I have got 'Thorndale' on board, which is a most comfortable
book."

Four days later, he wrote that he was able to
move his fingers, and the stitches were taken out
of his shoulder; and describes the cook, who in
running away had received two dreadful gashes
in the back, and could only lie on his stomach.
"Very lucky I did not turn round to bolt," he

says; "if so, must have been cut down from behind. I owe my life to Morison coming up when he did, and R. and L. owe their lives to my stopping the two men who were hurrying along the passage within three yards of their doors." His opinion was that after this assault, which the Japanese elaborately made out to be an expression of private hatred alone, and entirely unconnected with any official, the British Government had but two courses before it—the one a war with Japan, the other withdrawal at once and summarily. "I don't depart from my old theoretical views. The result of our forcing ourselves upon people who never wanted us, has been to place us in the dilemma from which the only escape is one or other of the courses I have proposed. If we are withdrawn, I shall feel very much my tail between my legs; if we go to war, I shall go in for looting daimios' palaces and feel a blackguard!"

Laurence discovered afterwards that the unaccountable ineffectiveness of his encounter with the Japanese ruffian was fully explained by the fact that the blows on both sides were rendered comparatively harmless by a great beam, which neither saw in the darkness, immediately over their heads, and on which the sword and hunting-whip respectively had expended their

blows. It was discovered to be slashed and
dinted with the sword-cuts which ought to have
killed the combatant on one side, and the blows
which ought to have felled the assailant on the
other. But for this it is almost impossible that
Oliphant in his night-dress, with his loaded
whip-handle, standing against an antagonist
in a mail-coat and with a sword, could have
escaped with his life. But in the meantime
the all-important moments during which he
kept back the assassins decided the failure
of the attempt. "I believe our escape was
mainly owing to the determined manner in
which your son kept our assailants at bay for
some time, till our guards came up," wrote one
of the *attachés* to Lady Oliphant; and I am
tempted to quote entire the letter of Bligh the
servant, who was ready to stand by his master to
the death, but who chilled the very blood in his
veins by his tragic whisper when the little group
stood waiting for the rush which they expected
every moment, "Do you think, sir, they will
torture us before they kill us?" Half fainting
from loss of blood, unable to defend himself
further whatever might happen, and with the
certainty in his mind that escape was impossible,
Laurence was lying in a chair, too dizzy and
weak to mind what was happening, when all

the blood remaining in his body was brought to
his brain by these words. "This horrible suggestion brought out a cold perspiration," he says;
"and I trust I may never again experience the
sensation of dread with which it inspired me."
Bligh's letter, however, was more considerate
than his speech.

"LADY OLIPHANT,—Believing a letter from me
just now would be acceptable, I take the earliest
opportunity. I have already disobeyed your commands in not writing before, for which I crave
pardon, and can only now say a few words about
the late occurrence. It was a very cowardly
assault, but fortunately without the results intended. You may be quite comfortable about
my master, whatever you hear to the contrary.
He has a slight wound on the shoulder, the right
side, and a cut on the left arm just above the
wrist, which I am very glad to say are doing
wonderfully well; and am very happy to add
my master's health is excellent, which, combined
with the care of the kind and attentive surgeon
of the Ringdove, with all due allowance for such
wounds, within three weeks or one month my
master will be himself again. He is very irrit-
able at not having a more deadly weapon than
the hunting-whip, so as to have floored his op-

ponent.   I believe had it not been for my master
stopping the fellows when he did, so gallantly
and quite unsupported, we should have had a
different tale to tell.   I may add, three or four
of the fellows were killed and as many taken.

"Hoping this short letter will meet your approbation, I beg to remain, your ladyship's humble
servant,   SAMUEL BLIGH."

This good fellow had been engaged in helping
his master to form an entomological collection for
the British Museum,—"running after butterflies,"
as Laurence describes.   They had found a rare
beetle, to their pride and joy, a day or two before ; and the tragic, half-seen, black figures, in-
vading the sleeping house in the dark, gave note
of their stealthy coming to Bligh by stumbling
over the tray full of sharp pins upon which the
insects were impaled — a curious mixture, half
comic, as so many tragic occurrences are.

It was considered right that Laurence should
return home with the news of the condition of
the embassy, and the necessity for taking some
decided steps to secure their safety and dignity,
or withdrawal—as soon as he was able to travel.
He had a curious commission on his way—to find
out and warn off a Russian man-of-war, which
had stolen into a secluded island-harbour in the

face of all treaties, and was then ensconced guilt-
ily in the shelter of the endless windings of the
waters, surveying and preparing for anything that
might happen in the future. Laurence was so far
recovered that he was able to carry out this commission with his usual coolness and success, and
caught the Russians, without warning, in this
curious secret employment. He returned home
within a few months from the time he left London, and he never again returned to the diplomatic service. He had only been about ten days
in his post : this was all the actual and formal
employment given him directly by the Government, without the intervention of any such powerful and friendly patron as Lord Elgin.

CHAPTER VII.

POLITICAL ADVENTURE—SOCIAL LIFE.

NOTWITHSTANDING the consequences of his wounds,
which he felt for some time—indeed he never fully
recovered the use of his left hand, several of the
fingers of which were permanently disabled—it
was not for long that Laurence could persuade
himself to keep still and recover his strength in
quiet. It is difficult to make out, from any certain information, whether he had some mission of
inquiry in hand, either from the Government or
the 'Times,' or was merely working on his personal impulse, with that thirst to know all the
intricacies of foreign politics which was always
strong in him, when he set out again, in the
leisure of his sick-leave, on a journey much more
serious than the usual wanderings of convales-
cence. I believe, however, I am right in saying
that many, if not all, of his apparently personal
travels at this period of his life were in reality

charged with a political object, and that his
wildest wanderings and farthest afield were in
the public service. It was his luck—a kind of
good fortune which was constantly befalling him
—to encounter at Vienna the Prince of Wales
and his suite, then, in the beginning of 1862,
on their way to the Holy Land, and to be invited to accompany them for a portion of their
way, as far as Corfu. The Prince of Wales was
then a very young man, and his character as yet
unknown to the nation, which has learnt to know
and esteem its fine qualities since then; and it is
interesting to read the early estimate of the royal
youth formed by so keen an observer :—

"As I had already been to all the places on the
Adriatic coast at which we touched, and was able
to do cicerone, I spent a most pleasant ten days,
at the same time doing a little quiet political
observation. I was delighted with the Prince,
and thought he was rarely done justice to in
public estimation : he is not studious nor highly
intellectual, but he is up to the average in this
respect, and beyond it in so far as quickness of
observation and general intelligence go. Travelling is, therefore, the best sort of education he
could have, and I think his development will be
far higher than people anticipate. Then his tem-

per and disposition are charming. His defects
are rather the inevitable consequences of his position, which never allows him any responsibility,
or forces him into action."

From Corfu Laurence crossed over the main-
land within the line of those blue mountains of
Albania, which rise with so much soft majesty
over the sea. The country was then, as perpet-
ually in its history, distracted with wars and
tumults, little comprehensible to the rest of the
world ; but which he was of opinion would one
time or another force themselves upon the general
consideration,—an opinion which those who are
acquainted with the commotions and revolutions
going on in the out-of-the-way corners of the
earth are very apt to entertain, since it seems
incredible that matters so momentous on the
scene of operations should not affect sooner or
later the larger mass of the body politic, the
band of nations which make up what we call the
world. "I was very much struck," he says,
"with the popular ignorance which prevailed in
this country in regard to the revolt in Bosnia
and Herzegovina, which finally led to the Russo-
Turkish war. At the outbreak of that movement,
the press, so far as I remember without an exception, assumed that it was a revolt of Chris-

tians against Turks, and I found the same impression existed even among members of the Cabinet; the fact being that it was an agrarian rising of Slav Christian peasants against Slav Moslem landlords, very much analogous in many aspects to our own landlord and tenant question in Ireland."

He does not, however, tell us on which side were his own sympathies, though he speaks of being the guest, in Herzegovina, of one of the landlords thus described. Whether it was with this rural dignitary, or with some expedition on the other side, that he himself went out to taste that whiff of war which he could never resist, there is no information. "We went out one day to do a little skirmishing," he says in the letter already quoted; "but we found the enemy, who had occupied the place in force the day before, had retired, so we had a 'walk over.' I found a great deal that was of political interest going on, or rather germinating, and indited a despatch accordingly. Nothing can be worse than the present condition of the Turkish provinces, and when taken in connection with the row, the prospect looks bad."

He was not then aware how much he would have to do with the Turkish sway in after-years, nor was he yet personally acquainted with that exasperation which it seems capable beyond all other governments (which is saying a great deal) of raising in the mind. The following curious anticipation would seem to have referred to some project of State which was never carried out: "I do not see how Venice is to be freed except at the price of the Ionian Isles. I know you don't care about that; but I think it is hardly fair that while the Emperor *makes* by freeing Italy, we should lose by the same transaction." Does this, one wonders, refer to some passing project of handing over the islands to Austria as a compensation for the loss of the Veneto: which changed into a determination to give them away to somebody, as often happens when a present is determined upon, and the first proposed recipient fails?

This expedition concluded with several amusing adventures, all set forth in the most charming way in chapter xii. of the 'Episodes.' On his way through the wild region of the Abruzzi, then scarcely known to travellers, and unsafe without a strong escort, he received in one instance an enthusiastic reception as the supposed nephew of Lord Palmerston; and in another came upon a most curious official, in the shape of the wife of the English vice-consul, who had been for some time exercising such small duties as appertained to his office, the husband having deserted her and his post simultaneously. But naturally this strange substitute was unable to act in the political business which Oliphant had in hand. It was here, too, in the little port of Manfredonia, that he received the following invitation : " Miss Thimbleby requests the pleasure of English gentleman's company to tea to-night at nine o'clock. Old English style ; " and accepting it, found a quaint little fossil of an Englishwoman, " very old, well on in the nineties," " a little old woman like a witch," with whom he drank tea solemnly, and to whom no doubt he made himself as delightful as if she had been young, beautiful, and a duchess. She was a sister of Mrs Jordan the actress, of all people in the world.

In a prison in one of the little towns which he visited, and where the captured brigands were the chief object of curiosity, Laurence saw " the beautiful wife of a notorious chief of one of the bands, who had been captured dressed in man's clothes, and using her pistol with such effect that she seriously wounded a soldier before she was taken prisoner,"—which incident no doubt suggested to him the extremely amusing story of the " Brigand's Bride," published some time afterwards in ' Blackwood's Magazine,' and re-

printed in a little volume called 'Fashionable
Philosophy.' It is not a tale which professes to
be authentic ; but the humorous dare-devil of the
story has a sufficient family resemblance to our
active explorer—who pushed his way everywhere,
feared nothing, and delighted above all in strange
and novel experiences of humanity — to make
him interesting, even with the fantastic acces-
sories of the air-gun, and the wondering tim-
orous population which is done to the life. It
is easy to imagine Laurence himself seated, like
his hero, outside the chemist's door, the usual
gossiping - place of the provincial Italian, with
the notary and doctor and priest and the
Sindaco of the little town, acute but ignorant,
hanging upon his lips, knowing nothing of
England but its greatness and the eccentricity
of the Inglese, and Palmerston the fetich of
the age; and receiving all the wonderful stories
told them with a faith tempered by surprise,
and the keenness of that Italian intelligence
which understands humour better than any
other Continental nation. The reader would
do well to take in the wild fun and extravagance of this story to the more sober record,
not as fact, but as a most amusing and vivid
illustration of the wanderer's possibilities, and
of that characteristic rural yet urban life. Now-

adays the traveller on his rush to India passes
Foggia and the other little towns of the coast
at something as near express speed as is possible in Italy — and no doubt they must have
gone through certain revolutions in consequence ;
but the gossips still sit round the apothecary's
door in the soft evenings, although some smat-
terings of knowledge may have penetrated, with
much politics and the newspaper, into their anti-
quated society.

On his return from this expedition it became
necessary for Laurence to decide whether he
should or should not return to his post in Japan.
The alternative was to do this or to retire altogether from the diplomatic service, and all the
hopes involved in it.   "It was with great regret,"
he says, " that I found myself compelled by family
considerations to adopt the latter alternative, and
abandon a career which had at that time peculiar
attractions for me, and in which, considering my
age, I had made rapid progress."   Had he returned to Japan, it would have been to the highly
important position of *chargé d'affaires*, which
could not have failed to lead to continuous and
profitable employment, and represented indeed
the ball at his foot so far as diplomatic service
was concerned ; but there can be little doubt
that the anxieties of his mother, after the dreadful

experience she had passed through at the time of his wound and illness, were not to be trifled with, and that it was in consideration for her very natural feelings that he gave up the far-distant and dangerous post.

It was one thing, however, to give up Japan, and another to give up the travel and adventure which were his very life; and accordingly not many months had elapsed before he was afloat again. "In January 1863 the Polish insurrection broke out; and as," he says with frank humour, "I had by this time acquired a habit of fishing in troubled waters, I determined to go and see it." Once more I must refer the reader to the 'Episodes' for the account of this interesting historical event. The evolutions of foreign politics are always difficult to follow, and the difficulty is largely increased when it is the outs and ins of popular feeling and the policy of an insurrection, even when so important as to be called a national movement, that are in question. Laurence penetrated into the councils of the unfortunate Poles, who were playing so tragic a game, and into one of the camps of the insurgents, a stray corps, pathetically small and defenceless, but animated by such a fire of enthusiasm as kindled the very heart of the spectator, open as that was to all generous sympathies. He made this visit at peril of his life, with a perfect consciousness that the Cossacks were very little discriminating, and would not have stopped to inquire what a wandering Englishman had to do *dans cette galère*, or to respect his nationality, had they chanced to come upon the little agitated party who had escorted him to the camp. He must, however, have had that confidence in his own fate which a man who has made a hundred hairbreadth escapes naturally has.

His picture of the camp in the woods, almost within hearing of a Russian army, where every man held his life in his hands, is singularly impressive and interesting. When the whole party united in the Polish national song, the effect was overwhelming.

"When all joined in the grand prayer to God which forms the swelling chorus, and the men, with swords drawn, uplifted their arms in supplication, the tears streamed down the cheeks of the women as they sang, for they remembered their sisters slain on their knees in the churches at Warsaw for doing the same, and bloody memories crowded on them, as, with voices trembling from emotion, they besought, in solemn strains, the mercy of the Most High. The scene was so full of dramatic effect that I scarcely believed in its reality till I remembered the existence of six thousand Russian soldiers in the immediate neighbourhood, who were thirsting for the blood of this little band of men and women. There was something practical in this consideration calculated to captivate a mind too prosaic to be stirred by theatrical representations; for I confess I find it generally more easy to delude myself by believing in the sham of a reality, than in the reality of a sham. However, upon this occasion he must have been a most uncompromising stoic who was not touched and impressed."

I quote the above passage chiefly from the curious little bit of self-disclosure which betrays the Scotch nationality of a man so cosmopolitan. Many Englishmen, and almost every Scot, will sympathise with this suspiciousness in respect to theatrical circumstances and instinctive horror of the sham, which sometimes reacts upon his appreciation of the true. That this keen intuitive criticism should exist in a spirit open to every enthusiasm and full of sympathy, in this particular case, may astonish those who are not familiar with that remarkable and most interesting development; and it all throws a very singular light upon his own after-career.

In the course of the same year, after a brief

return to England, Laurence once more set out
for the same distant and little-known region.
The portion of his correspondence which refers
to this period of his life has not fallen into my
hands; but there is no doubt that all these repeated journeys had their distinct political object,
and were far from being the mere adventures they
seem. Only a short time had elapsed since his
previous visit, and yet it was long enough to
permit the downfall of the Polish hopes, the im-
prisonment and death of many of the friends who
had then received him, and the all but suppression
of the revolt. As it still lived, however, in out-
of-the-way corners, and still entertained pathetic
hopes, never to be fulfilled, of French or English
intervention, the deep interest which Oliphant
felt in the brave men who had welcomed him so
kindly, impelled him to another visit, though the
expedition was full of risk. He was accompanied
by a friend, the Hon. Evelyn Ashley, and their
object was to penetrate into the Russian prov
inces of Volhynia, where it was believed that
revolution was smouldering, if not yet accompanied by any perceptible blaze. It is curious
that he should thus have made his way over
ground which, many years after, he was again
to traverse in the interests of the Jews—a people
who did not in any degree commend themselves

to him during this first journey. The attempt to
penetrate into the disaffected province was, however, wholly ineffectual; and after some adventures, which are amusing enough in the narrative though far from amusing in the experience,
the Englishmen were turned back, and made a
masterly retreat to Jassy, where, on the invitation of a nun encountered in a box at the opera
—a most remarkable scene for such a meeting—
Laurence and his companion made a most amusing and picturesque tour in Moldavia, proceeding
from one convent to another, each more piquant
and interesting than the one preceding it, in
which companies of recluses lived in the most
liberal and uncontrolled manner, the nuns, like
Flemish Beguines, in little cottages picturesquely
grouped together, and both monks and nuns surrounded by blooming gardens, and much that was
calculated to make life agreeable. This was perhaps the only detour among many journeys which
had no political meaning, though it furnished a
most agreeable article for 'Blackwood' and a delightful chapter in the 'Episodes.'

At the end of this pleasant break in his exciting life, he turned his steps northwards in another
direction where trouble was brewing, always the
greatest attraction, notwithstanding his keen enjoyment of every novelty in human life. This

time it was to Schleswig-Holstein, then enveloped
in the smoke and fumes of a contention which nobody at least within our four seas understood,
that he went to study the disputed succession
and all the questions involved. "As confessedly
it was one which the British statesmen of the
day considered beyond their comprehension, and
as the British public never even tried to understand it, it was no wonder that our policy was
mistaken throughout. When a question has more
than two sides, the popular intelligence fails to
grasp it. As most questions of foreign policy
have generally three at least, and sometimes
more, and as Ministers are compelled to adopt
the popular view if they wish to retain office,
the foreign policy of England is usually charac-
terised by a charming simplicity, not always con-
ducive to the highest interests of the country."

The question in this case was a triangular one,
the little Schleswig-Holstein desiring its own
sovereign and a peaceable small independence,
while spectators at a distance considered the conflict to be one between the Danes and Prussians
for the possession of a coveted morsel of which
the nationality was just doubtful enough to give
to each a certain claim. In the distant eddies
of opinions in those days I remember that the
French Government was warmly censured for not

taking energetic action on behalf of the Poles, their traditionary allies and *protégés*, while Great Britain was equally blamed for not interfering to defend the rights of the Danes. I recollect overhearing upon the deck of a steamboat on the lake of Como an animated discussion on the subject between some Italian gentlemen, whose energetic denunciation of the British Government as "un governo infame," in consequence of their desertion of Denmark, was loud and vigorous. Laurence, however, held a very different view : his sympathies were with neither of the greater contending parties, but for the Duke of Sonderburg-Augustenburg, whose claims were overlooked on both sides.

This was the last of these purely political adventures in which a thirst for information, the desire of novelty and excitement, and a certain ambition to know thoroughly and make himself an authority upon the most complicated questions of European politics, were the ostensible motives. Though he is always individual and interesting in whatever he writes, the hundred little personal revelations of his private correspondence are wanting in these bustling but unproductive years, in which he seems to have worked off a great deal of superabundant energy, and gradually calmed and settled down into a state of mind adapted to residence at home, and the routine of ordinary English life. He was now, in 1864, when he returned to England from the battle which settled the fate of Schleswig-Holstein, a man of thirty-five, in the height of life and faculty, with an extraordinary knowledge of the world and mankind. The reader may think, perhaps, that such experiences as those of Japan and Circassia were not entirely adapted to form him for the localities of Mayfair and St Stephen's. It must, however, be remembered that between his journeys there had interposed on many occasions a slice of society, usually at its most animated and gayest moment; that he knew everybody at home as well as abroad,— British Ministers as well as Chinese mandarins, literary circles as well as political, and fashionable circles better than either; that he had friends everywhere, among both small and great, and was acquainted with English life to its depths, but especially with the representative classes which we call the "world,"—and in which the brightest intelligence and grace, as well as the most perfect frivolity and foolishness, are to be found. He knew these classes, understood their importance and their worth, and scorned their social superiority while esteeming it, in full consciousness of the paradox which existed both in them and in himself. He saw through every social pretence with the keenest glance of intelligence and humour, and never hesitated to impale any offender upon his shining spear, or laugh at any absurdity; yet instinctively held by that world to which, satirist and revolutionary as he was, he belonged, and felt himself at home in it, as he never was in less distinguished but possibly more genuine spheres. This curious distinction was never more clearly evidenced than in Laurence Oliphant's life. He was not rich : his ancient race had never been of great pretensions, or with claims beyond the modest gentlehood of the county to which it belonged : yet his standing-ground throughout his life was that of society ; and the world of fashion, though he mocked it continually, and shot a thousand darts at its mannerisms and follies, was, after all, his natural sphere.

It was in the year 1864 that Laurence returned home more or less " for good," with the determination of finding, if possible, settled employment in England, or at least carving out some occupation for himself which would permit him to have a settled home there, and relieve and cheer his mother's loneliness. I think her comfort must have been his great motive in this determination, and perhaps, too, a little disgust with the public service in distant parts of the earth, where the best efforts of one representative of England were apt to be altogether discredited by the actions of another, or by misadventure, or by Government neglect, as happened in the case of Lord Elgin—whose proceedings were subjected to endless animadversion as incomplete and unsatisfactory, as soon as the next difficulty with China arose. The interval which elapsed between Oliphant's return from his late wanderings and his election to Parliament was most actively and fully taken up, although he held no appointment; and what between literature, society, lectures—which he seems to have given in many places, generally with a view to the future election — and visits, his mind at this time was fully occupied. He had always, or almost always, a book preparing for the press, always a round of country-houses attending his leisure, always a hundred engagements in town. I find a succession of letters recounting the experiences of one autumn, which I at first concluded to belong to this period, difficult as the chronology is always, for his correspondence as usual is completely destitute of dates, but which in reality belongs to the conclusion of 1859, after his first China expedition. However, it does very well as an example of how his autumns were generally spent, and the reader will, I hope, admit the retrospective glance.

He was coquetting with various constituencies at the time, in a series of experiences, repeated a few years later; hoping to move the heart of Glasgow, but not unwilling to content himself with Greenock, and with a steadfast eye upon the Stirling burghs, as the sober certainty upon which he could always fall back. His letters are full of amusing sketches of the people among whom he moved; from the lively and distinguished visitors in country-houses to the chance companions he picked up in railway carriages, of one of whom, for example, he writes : "Had a delightful journey, my companion being a young man from London in the wholesale woollen and stuff trade, from whom I derived much useful information." This "delightful journey" carried him to Sir James Clarke's house of Birk Hall, where he met "a most learned and delightful party (including Professor Owen, Sir Charles Lyell, and various others of the same calibre), all *savants* of the first water, and consequently most agreeable and entertaining society. I wish I could always live in it." The leap from the young man in the woollen trade to these high potentates is long enough; but they were equally interesting to his always eager and lively intelligence, and nothing could give a better idea of his universal interest in human life and character.

The occasion on which he met this delightful party was a meeting of the British Association at Aberdeen, where he took a considerable share in the proceedings, along with Captain Sherard Osborn, Captain Speke, and other travellers of authority, and read a paper in the Geographical Section upon Japan, which was at the period his special subject. He gave as usual a brief, but lively, description of this to his mother in London :

" I wish you had cared as little for the ordeal of reading a paper as I did. There was nothing on earth to be nervous about. The hall was crowded to the door, and they listened with great attention for the forty minutes which my paper lasted, and cheered me vociferously when it was over, so I suppose it pleased them. I have promised to lecture at Leeds on the state of our political relations with China. If I can't say what I want in the House of Commons, I must find some other place. I will get it fully reported in the ' Times.' "

Other proposals to the same effect poured upon him. He was asked to Glasgow to discourse :

at one time to the merchants in the Chamber of Commerce, "who are coming in a select body to hear me, a regular business lecture," "no ladies admitted," he adds regretfully; at another to the Young Men's Christian Association. "I shall have treated Japan in every variety of way before I have done," he says. He had also lectures to deliver at Dunfermline, at Stirling, at Greenock, and was invited by the Philosophical Institution in Edinburgh to deliver two, all on the same subject of Japan. The last proposal was accompanied by an offer of £20 for the two lectures, which does not seem a large sum, but which he considers "not to be despised." He was also moved by the fact that "only distinguished men lectured there, and the audience is large and important." "I never expected to turn popular lecturer," he says; "I have not sought to be pushed forward in this way, but seeing that I am without any special occupation in London, I think I ought to do what comes to my hand." He had, besides, the strong inducement of a desire "to get hold of Glasgow," "which would give me a position in the House of Commons," he says, "above what a young man could expect." And indeed there seem to have been vague negotiations on this subject, invitations to stand from " a Glasgow body," whom he evidently considered without sufficient authority. Laurence desired nothing more than to be asked to stand ; but he was wise enough not to commit himself, even on the warrant of his enthusiastic reception, and the compliments of the Glasgow potentates, while the fumes of his lecture were still in their heads. At Greenock he had an amusing experience, which I think he describes in one of his books, but of which I will quote the report to his mother, at first hand. He was disappointed and half offended on arriving to find no one in waiting to meet him, and to have to find his way by himself to the hotel.

" However, the secretary came at last to show me the way to the Free Kirk where I was to lecture. Dunlop was not in the chair, having been detained in Edinburgh, so the sheriff presided instead. I was somewhat dismayed to find myself mounting the steps of a very high pulpit, and looking down upon the upturned faces of about twelve hundred people, who crammed the church to overflowing ; still more dismayed to hear the minister, who occupied the precentor's desk beneath me, call upon the congregation to join him in prayer—which was a very long one, a great part of it personal to myself, and asking

a blessing upon the discourse I was about to
enter upon. I began to think I would try my
hand at a sermon, as the lecture I was going to
give was likely to be far too full of jokes to be
appropriate to the occasion. However, I dis-
coursed at starting on Japan as a field for missionary enterprise, and then, finding I had a
sympathetic audience, I was more light and
airy, until at last I kept them all in a highly
amused condition. I looked over my red pulpit
cushion and saw the old minister giggling immensely. Altogether I think it was the most
successful lecture I have given. I despise even
notes now, and find practice is improving my
delivery. Nor did I feel the least fatigued.
Four of the leading people were profuse in their
apologies afterwards for the coolness of my reception, which they declared was a mistake. I
am to go a round of visits with one of them
this morning."

These coquettings with the busy towns and
cities of the west of Scotland did not, however,
come to anything; and when the decisive moment
arrived, it was to Stirling, where his name itself
was a recommendation and his family so well
known, that he turned. He had already contested these burghs, unsuccessfully but hope-

fully, before going to China — an incident of
which I find scarcely any record except of the
mere fact, and that he had much enjoyed the
business of canvassing, in which his father,
also greatly amused and excited, as was the
character of the family, had helped and accompanied him. His reflections on this subject,
on a renewed visit to Stirling, are touching
and full of feeling. He gives an account of a
brief visit to Stirling on his way to Broomhall,
the home of Lord Elgin, and his meeting with
his former agents :—

"They declare they can bring me in against
Caird next time, if I wish it. The few of my
old supporters whom I saw are most enthusiastic. I have a strong body of friends in Stirling. I feel quite melancholy in renewing all
these associations, however : they recall papa so
vividly to my mind. He has been so warmly
mentioned by several persons to me. They got
to like him so much. M'Farlane says that the
look of him as he walked down the street got
me votes."

This pretty and very Scotch touch of affectionate hyperbole is affecting, between the smile
and the tear, and was no doubt spoken with

water in the eyes of the plain Stirling "writer" so unexpectedly poetical.

As a background to these public appearances, comes a lively and shifting panorama of Scotch country-houses, in which there are many vivid glimpses of individual character and manners. Laurence was not superior to gossip on occasion, as perhaps it is impossible for a man so full of interest in his fellow-creatures to be ; but he had not time or inclination to send to his mother anything more than a rapid *aperçu* here and there of the individualities with which he was brought into contact. There is but one case, I think, in which a private and painful imbroglio of real life is referred to ; and in that case both mother and son were actively employed in smoothing down and clearing up the unfortunate difficulty, in the course of which the young man gives vent to various judgments upon the impossibility of Platonic attachments, for instance (afterwards the chief doctrine and belief of his life), which are very authoritative and decided ; but offers himself, as few men would be likely to do, as the agent to bring "the man," the disturber of domestic happiness, to reason, and to convince him, not without reference to his own (Laurence's) private experiences, of the necessity of absolute withdrawal.

I am happy to say, however, that, in con-
tradistinction to so many series of correspondence that have been made open to the world,
there is no scandal, no piquant stories, no indis-
cretions or betrayals, in these ever lively and
graphic letters. If he sometimes speaks in his
books as if he believed all society to be corrupt,
he finds, as a sane and wholesome man should do,
no trace of corruption in the households that receive him—nothing but points of character, cheerful indications of identity, something to like and
to please everywhere. As usual, the young ladies
call for a great deal of his attention, and "a walk
with the lassies" in the afternoon, after he has
got through his work, was a very favourite amusement. Indeed there is a little glamour of easy
sentiment in his eyes as he goes from one circle
to another, always ready for a touch of pleasant
emotion, and by no means unwilling to be awakened to deeper feelings. "I am deeply in love
with them all," he says of a bevy of pretty sisters,
which no doubt was consolatory to the mind of
the mother, always uneasy on this point. One
lady, whom he had already admired and specu-
lated a little upon, is more particularly discussed.
Some one has been describing her to him in the
highest terms. "She has a charming disposition,
thoroughly unselfish—but muckle hands and feet!

What is that, you will say, to good mental qualities?   I don't think she is the least brilliant, but
with very good common-sense. In fact, she would
suit you perfectly. As for myself, I despair of
finding any one ; probably when I do, she will be
an aversion unto you."

While thus living with his work and his lectures, and his afternoon walk with the "lassies"
of the house, his reports of himself are exceedingly
cheerful : " Whenever I can dispose of my time to
my own satisfaction between innocent recreation
and profitable employment, I am happy ; but,
when employment is wanting, the recreation often
ceases to be innocent, 'Satan finding some mischief
still,' &c.   And when the recreation is wanting,
as in Edinburgh, I become low-spirited and de-
pressed."

The light-hearted reports of his letters inform
us—at second-hand through his mother—of such
incidents as his performances at a tenants' ball in a
house where he " danced reels violently till 3 A.M.,
and woke so fresh at seven that I wrote my book
till eleven o'clock, when the rest of the knocked-
up world at last came to breakfast ": how he
gravely interviewed a young man in an office who
" wants me to put him in the same line of life I
have followed myself, as he hates the writer's
desk ; but I don't know how that is to be done."

How he discusses theology everywhere whenever he has a chance, "exchanging 'Thorndale' with Lady A. for two of Maurice's works"; and finding a great *savant* "utterly off the line in secret, and confirmed by recent geological discoveries, but he is afraid to publish. I urged him strongly to go in for truth, *ruat cœlum*. He said, 'Nobody with less than £3000 a-year can afford to hold my views,'" which does not say very much for the philosopher. All this shows the versatility of mind with which he leaped lightly from one subject to another, with a lively interest in all. He was not disposed, I am sorry to say, to church-going, professing "a terrible tendency to ague in the draughts of country churches, but not saying anything about a much greater dread which I have of country parsons." Once at a service of the kind called Puseyite in those days, he declared it to be "like badly got-up Buddhism." He describes a popular clergyman of the time as "a man with the mind of a woman and the voice of a trumpet, very aggravating but amiable." But on the occasion of a visit to Glasgow, he declares with much warmth, "Norman Macleod is a trump. He and Guthrie are the only decent parsons I know." His enjoyment of the life thus described is very clearly set forth in one of his letters, and all its delights, not without a little natural complacence, while yet he anticipates with philosophy the need for settling down in a more humble way :—

"My life is necessarily (in general) a good deal made up of excitements and reactions; for instance, just now here I am scarcely able to turn, for a press both of business and pleasure. Half-a-dozen lectures to prepare, proofs constantly to correct, and book not yet finished. Charming women at hand when I am inclined for a cosy chair in the drawing-room and a touch of the æsthetic. Any amount of game merely for the trouble of strolling through a few turnip-fields : A. and I killed twenty - one brace of partridges the day before yesterday. Any number of horses to ride—all the more to be appreciated after two years of filth, heat, and absence of social and intellectual enjoyment. But I hope I shall not be such a goose as to growl at London because I have enjoyed myself here. If I see my way to being comfortably independent, and am allowed that amount of personal liberty which, from being so much my own master, I am accustomed to, I think you will find me a happy and contented companion in our lodging, even though occupation and pleasure are both suddenly slack. I should be more than ungrateful if I were not thankful for the blessing of having you to share it with me."

That this sentiment was thoroughly sincere, every line of his letters testifies; but yet there were times when his mother's continual anxiety to have his "serious thoughts," as well as the lighter record of his sayings and doings, communicated to her, brings a momentary touch of half-comic irritation. "You must be philosophical as to the condition of my spiritual being," he says; and while telling her of one after another of the great ladies, his friends, who desire to make her acquaintance, and whose somewhat puzzled admiration of the close bond between mother and son is apparent, he adds an amusing story told him by one of them, of a certain old Lady Campbell who had, like Lady Oliphant, one dearly beloved and perfect son but no more. "One day at prayers, when the minister was saying, 'For there is no good in us, and we are every one of us miserable sinners,' she was heard audibly to protest, 'Oh, no' my Airchy, no' my Airchy!'" The application was easy.

The year 1865, however, forms a definite era in his life. His wanderings, his vagaries of mind and thought, even his impatience with the imperfections of so-called religious persons and desire of finding some better way, had plunged him during the two or three previous years more and more, whenever it was within his reach, into the

excitement of society, which was at once an anti-
dote to the restlessness of thought, and which
the attitude he repeatedly compares to that of
Mr Micawber, of waiting for something to turn
up, made a necessity to him.   For where was he
to find the patron, the appointment on which his
mind was set, save among the great personages,
holders of power and influence, who were to be
met with there?   I do not pretend to be able
to give a history of his social experiences during
the intervals when he reappeared in London, always with the *éclat* of some new performance or
event — the successes of China, the hairbreadth
escape of Japan, the mysterious politics of mid-
Europe—something always fresh and unknown, to
surround him with attraction.   Probably it involved episodes of another kind from those of
adventure, and in which his heart was more
deeply concerned ; and it is by no means unlikely that, on the eve of a great religious
change, the current of his life may have run
more high in other directions, and the impetus
of existence at its fullest force have carried him
further than conscience approved—thus adding a
deeper need to the necessity always felt of a new
foundation, and a sharper point to his prevailing
consciousness of the imperfections in him and
about him, the hollowness of social pretences,

and the difficulty of holding the right way in a
society which condoned moral failure so easily, and
was only inexorable to poverty and social defeat.

In this year, however, these wanderings and
waitings came to an end, and Laurence's election
as member for the Stirling burghs fixed his residence in town, and seemed to all his friends the
beginning of a brilliant and useful career. That he
had every endowment and faculty likely to make
his new position a satisfactory one need scarcely
be said. He was no recluse, likely to be intimi-
dated by that so-called "august assembly,"—he
had full habit and usage of the world, and was
thoroughly acquainted with the atmosphere of
political life. The reasons which brought about
another result, and the disappointment of many
of the hopes conceived by his friends, if not
by himself, will become apparent further on. I
cannot doubt that he was pleased with the new
beginning of life, at least in its first stage. It
had been in his mind from the very commence-
ment of his career as the alternative to the life of
diplomacy, which was what had commended itself
to him most. And he took it up heartily, hoping
to play an important part in the history of his
country. He had contested the Stirling burghs
once, if not twice, before,—the first time while
still very young, in his father's lifetime, before

the China expedition,—and he had many humourous stories to tell of the incidents of his canvassing. One of these, of which a friend tells me, describes how he was taken to one person of influence after another, the most important of all being a cobbler, ensconced in a dark little shop approached by two or three steps leading downwards below the level of the street. Here he underwent the process of "heckling" with much severity, and was put through his political catechism so entirely to the satisfaction of the shoemaker politician, that he smote the candidate upon the shoulder in the intensity of his satisfaction, exclaiming, "You're the billie for me!"

This event was to all appearance and human likelihood the beginning of a mature and established life. It was in reality no such thing, but only a transition period—a temporary pause and point between the life which he had lived like other men, and another so unique and extraordinary as to separate him from all his fellows. But this time of transition was in itself signalised by so much that was brilliant and remarkable in the development of his mind and genius, as to form a special and most important chapter in his career. His intellect seemed to have reached a sudden climax of energy, wit, and power, and his whole nature burst forth in an overflow of gifts which hitherto had been restrained in channels inappropriate to their full exhibition,—in a kind of riot of fancy, fun, and satirical brilliancy and insight, of which he had given scarcely any indication before.

This extraordinary new outburst, in which all the fire of contending elements long smouldering in him rose into sudden flame, was preceded by an undertaking, briefly alluded to in the 'Episodes,' and very unique in its way, which may be taken more or less as the conclusion of his entirely mundane career. He had never been one of the " worldly holies " of his own brilliant classification, nor was he ever at any time reckoned among those who affect superiority to the world, and thank God that they are not as other men ; but yet the distinction between the two portions of his life is very marked, though as paradoxical as ever. He was never so cynical in expression, so dazzling in satire, as when his whole life was disorganised by the new impulse which moved him to live for humanity and take love for the race of mankind as his only inspiration ; nor so wild in his apparent vagaries as when he first became conscious of an anchor in the unseen, and a certainty of conviction and established standing-ground.

It was, however, before he had altogether

opened to this new development that the singular and romantic (if such a word can be applied in such a sense) little venture of the 'Owl'—projected in laughter and high spirits, and carried out as an excellent joke by everybody concerned—was tossed into the mystified and astonished world. He explains its first beginning by a few words in respect to the exceptional position he had made for himself by his perpetual travels and political adventures. He had friends everywhere throughout the civilised (and indeed we may add the half-civilised) world, and in all the quarters which he had visited and studied, plunging into the troubled waters whenever he had a chance, and mastering every political combination he could push his way into; and from these friends over all the world he was in the habit of receiving communications on the exciting subjects which had brought them together. "For instance," he says, "a conference was at that time sitting in London on the Schleswig-Holstein question, consisting of plenipotentiaries of all the European Powers who had been parties to the Treaty of London, the proceedings at which were kept absolutely secret; yet a few days after each meeting, I received from abroad an accurate report of everything that had transpired at it—and this, I hasten to say,

through no one connected with our own Foreign
Office. I felt bursting with all sorts of valuable
knowledge, with no means of imparting it in a
manner which suited me."

It was in these circumstances that "a little
dinner" was given at a little house in Mayfair,
the residence of ladies who were great friends
of Oliphant's, and through him exceedingly hos-
pitable to various other young men of his immediate intimacy, all in the fullest current of
society and energy of life. I have heard one of
them say regretfully that such conversation as
that of this little *salon*—in which every man did
his best to shine, and to win the smile of a
hostess full of wit and brilliancy, and capable
herself of a full share in the *bon mots* that flew
about, and the discussions that took place between whiles—it has seldom been his lot to hear.
Amid the brilliant talk on this particular occasion it was suggested by some one "that a little
paper should be started by way of a skit, in
which the most outrageous *canards* should be
given as serious, and serious news should be
disguised in a most grotesque form." No doubt
the merry party began its composition on the
moment, with all the eagerness of a new amusement, and the *canards* made their first flight
over the bright dinner-table, with an additional

touch of colour laid on to each wing as they flitted
from *convive* to *convive*. They had the means
not only of dazzling and mystifying a dull public,
but also of getting at that public, which often
fails to such amusing projects ; for one of the company was Sir Algernon Borthwick, who " kindly
undertook to print the absurd little sheet."

The gay conspirators watched, with all the
gusto which attends a mystification, to see how
the jest took.   And it took like wildfire.   The
world got note of it while it was still damp
from the press, and soon in all the circles they
frequented, amid affairs of state, and the last
great scandal or discovery of the day, there rose
a murmur of inquiries, of guesses, and discussions
about this little droll solemn invader of society,
which knew everything, and had the secrets of
the Foreign Office at its finger-ends, and confounded and tantalised everybody with its extraordinary acquaintance with life and events.
It was the most excellent joke to the young
men.   When they saw carriages thronging the
street in which was the little shabby office from
which the ' Owl' was issued, they stole aside into
corners to laugh till they could laugh no more—
and in the evening eyed each other over the shoulders of the fashionable mob with twinkling eyes,
while all the great men and all the fine ladies

asked each other, What was the 'Owl'? Who
had communicated to it those startling secrets?
Where did it get its information? When the
plotters discovered that they were actually making money by the jest which they all enjoyed
so thoroughly, their amusement and satisfaction
became more piquant still; but in faithful ad-
herence to their original principle, they determined to spend their profit gaily,—not putting
it away in any dull banking account, but dedi-
cating it to a weekly dinner of the most sumptuous description, and other "larks." One of the
surviving members of this brilliant band tells
me of a great entertainment offered by the Owls
to all the "smart" ladies of their acquaintance,
when jewelled gifts were hung among the flowery
ornaments on the table, and all was harmony
and splendour, the whole defrayed by the fun
and wisdom of the eccentric journal, which
appeared when it pleased, always affording
society a new surprise. It is scarcely necessary
to say, however, that Laurence Oliphant did not
follow the career of this wild little bandit of the
press for any long continuance. He was a large
contributor to the first numbers, and continued
until the tenth. Then, or soon after, he found
the other contributors in the mind to adopt a
more business-like arrangement for what was in

the beginning pure sport, and he retired altogether from the undertaking. It continued its
career, I believe, for some years, appearing more
regularly, although only during the season, and
falling into more ordinary lines; for, to be sure,
neither mystification nor "larks" could continue
for ever.

Perhaps it was the success of this venture, so
far out of the usual decorous habitudes of the
press, which had not then fallen into the evil
ways of "Society" papers, which turned the
thoughts of Laurence to another use of the remarkable gifts of social satire and criticism, which
probably he himself became acquainted with in a
sort of surprise as well as his readers. Even in
the letters I have quoted, though they are always full of humorous touches, there are perhaps
fewer shafts of satirical description than could
be extracted from half the confidential letters
written from country - houses in any autumnal
season. And the books he had hitherto published
were entirely descriptive and political, full of
information and facts, though handled with so
light a hand, and pervaded by such an airy wealth
of amused and amusing observation, that they
read, as people say, "like a novel." But it was
altogether a new beginning when the traveller,
the diplomate, the serious spectator of distant

countries and political intrigues, suddenly per-
ceived that round about him—within the radius
of that mile of streets in which, for a part of the
year, there lives and feasts and dances and talks,
a community quite unconscious, in the simplicity
of its assumption, of any arrogance in calling itself
the World—lay boundless material for satire and
fancy. The inconsistency of people calling themselves Christians had long been a favourite subject
of indignant remark and criticism to Laurence, as
has been repeatedly noted already—perhaps too
favourite a subject, since to judge a system, and
particularly a belief, not on its own merits but
on those of the people who profess it, is scarcely
either fair or logical. But when or how it first
occurred to him, with a flash of sudden inspiration, that he possessed, hitherto unnoticed in his
armoury, a sharp - edged weapon of the kind of
Ithuriel's spear, upon which he could pick up and
exhibit, impaled upon its shining point, not only
to the world but to themselves, the masquerades
of society, I have been unable to discover, unless
the 'Owl' was the instrument of revelation. In
his letters to the editor of ' Blackwood's Magazine,'
in which the first number of ' Piccadilly,' published as a serial in that Magazine during the
summer of 1865, appeared, the doubtful character
of the entirely new venture—whether it would be

successful or not, whether it might merit success, how the world would receive it—are discussed with all the uncertainty of a beginner. It had occurred to me as quite possible that it was the suggestion of the able and far-seeing editor referred to, the late Mr John Blackwood, whose literary perceptions (though he never touched a pen save to write letters) were singularly trustworthy, which directed Oliphant to the unthought-of medium of fiction. And I find on inquiry that this was indeed partly the case, Mr Blackwood having mentioned to him a similar project on the part of J. G. Lockhart, the son-in-law and biographer of Sir Walter Scott, which probably acted as a spark to the ready fire of Laurence's as yet undisclosed thoughts. The first intimation of the work occurs as follows:—

"LONDON, *Jan.* 24, 1865.

"I enclose the MS. according to your wish. I am glad you think I might succeed in this kind of work. You will see from reading it what my idea was, one entirely 'novel,' and which could only be done in a serial—that is, to write a novel in the form of a contemporaneous autobiography, in which I should parody the incidents of the month, make my hero make speeches on public questions in the House of

Commons, stay in country-houses, flirt, shoot *à
la* Burnaby if need be, lecture, argue, &c. But
the difficulty is the plot: I cannot proportion the
importance of the plot and the opinions. I am
always losing sight of the former, being extremely
full of the latter. Then they are what would be
called extravagant in many points, and I don't
know that you would like to publish them. I
feel disposed to go in against most of the popular
ideas of the day, and utterly ignore existing prejudices on many serious matters; therefore the
chief aim would be to point a moral, with a vengeance. I am afraid of doing it too seriously,
and yet I don't want to bring it into ridicule by
too much burlesque. . . . The whole thing is
an experiment, not only in its chronology, but in
its other features. In the first place, it is a cari-
cature, and not intended to be quite natural or
possible. I look upon it as the highest form of
art to supplant the natural with the imaginative;
but of course it runs the risk of failing by reason
of its extravagance. My difficulty in the present
undertaking is to keep the grotesque element
within bounds: it is like a strong spice, the
flavour of which easily overpowers. As a sort of
qualification to this, I have determined on making Vanecourt more or less mad. In this character he becomes intensely interesting to draw,

and the play of his mind is a good study. Moreover, it enables his opinions and acts to be extravagant and inconsistent always, based, nevertheless, upon truth and rectitude, which two principles are so extremely dry and distasteful that nobody would care about a novel conveying such an old-fashioned moral unless it were put in some newfangled form. Nevertheless, I am quite sure the first parts, at all events, will mystify the public, and set up everybody's back. I shall consider it only a success if it is the best abused novel out. I see some of the reviewers think it is O'Dowd."

That all plans of this kind are much modified in the progress of the work is very rapidly perceptible. In no operation is the *solvitur ambulando* so strikingly manifested. "The best laid schemes o' mice and men" go astray nowhere so completely as in the working out of fiction. Only a few weeks have elapsed when Laurence writes again : "I get so interested in writing it that I feel it difficult to keep it waiting for events, so that the contemporaneous element will perhaps in course of time give way to the story, but that won't matter." As a matter of fact, neither the contemporaneous element (so soon out of date and forgotten) nor the story are the points that took

all readers by storm in 'Piccadilly.' The startling types of character—the worldly holy and
the wholly worldly : Lady Broadhem, with her
high principles in religion and her absolute, almost innocent, obtuseness to the first principles
of honesty in speculation ; the Stock Exchange
fashionable, Spiffy Goldtip, perhaps the earliest
revelation of that strange nondescript and auda-
cious schemer ; the bold yet abject parvenus ; the
mob of fashion, carried hither and thither as the
secret impulse was given—were its greatest attractions. Even the muscular colonial Bishop,
Joseph Caribbee Islands, the curious American
(a type very rampant in those days, now obso-
lete), and the converted Hindoo, though exceedingly amusing, were less heeded, being less tremendous in their exposition of reality and sham,
than the other terrible yet airy sketches, so light,
so powerful, almost tragical in satire, so true to
life.

"The fact is," the author adds, "that the
class which would appreciate it are not a maga-
zine-reading class. If it went down at all, it
would be entirely among the fashionables, who
never read serials or much else, and who would
read this because it came home to them. It
would go exactly where the 'Owl' did, to the
young ladies and people who never read news-

papers. When it got well talked of by the *beau monde*, the 'middles' would buy it—not because they would understand it, but because it would be the correct thing." Perhaps he was a little contemptuous here, as not unfrequently happens, of the "middles," among which highly indefinite and widely extended class there are plenty of Lady Broadhems, and the worldly holy flourish largely. But it was Society which was hit, and in the very centre of the shield.

"As for hurting me in the House, nothing," he says, "can hurt me, provided what I do is from a right motive. My only fear about my motive in this instance is that I may have a lurking vanity in it; but the motive I try to have is to wake people up, and make them either believe or disbelieve, and not go on humbugging with Providence any longer. If I am single and earnest in this, I defy all efforts to injure me anywhere." "I do feel that the times are so bad that they require exposure." These arguments in defence of his book are taken from letters to his publisher, who, it is curious to find, hesitated to republish as a book this extraordinarily brilliant work, to my mind the most powerful of all Oliphant's productions. "It is a great tax upon your friendship," Laurence says, "to ask you to do what you feel so disagreeable.

This has weighed very much with me ; but as
you say, ' If you are very much bent upon it, I
am willing,' I confess I am." This hesitation,
afterwards justified by the fact that ' Piccadilly,'
though a great literary success, was scarcely so in
a commercial point of view, had its share in keeping back the republication of the book, which—
notwithstanding the effect it produced on its appearance in ' Blackwood's Magazine,' even when its
daring assault upon the world was broken by the
intervals of publication, and it was still possible
for the Solomons of the newspapers to " think it
was O'Dowd "—was not produced in a permanent
form until five years had come and gone, bringing with them many strange revolutions, and
none more strange than those which had taken
place in the fortune of the author. That extraordinary crisis in the meantime altered everything for him,—who was, at the time ' Piccadilly '
was first printed, the man we know, newly
elected member of Parliament, one of the first
authorities upon foreign politics, the favourite of
society, the friend of all that was best and highest in England, a courted guest, a brilliant writer
and still more delightful conversationalist, capable
almost of any advancement : and who was, at the
time of its republication, no more than a visitor
in the brilliant circles which had before been his

home, with hands hardened by manual toil, a career thrown back into the regions of the accidental, and all advancement, as the word is generally understood, put away from both life and possibility. How such a wonderful change took place has now to be told. The reader who has followed his career so far will be able to foresee that it was at all times a possible thing that this might happen, and that the latent spark of the revolution had been lying for years in his heart, awaiting the hand that should stir it into life.

END OF THE FIRST VOLUME.

PRINTED BY WILLIAM BLACKWOOD AND SONS, EDINBURGH.

www.ingramcontent.com/pod-product-compliance
Lightning Source LLC
Chambersburg PA
CBHW060527030726
47498CB00004B/1100